Perpetual Mania

Landon Cook

Published by Landon Cook, 2024.

PERPETUAL MANIA

First edition. May 15, 2024.

ISBN: 979-8224948222

Written by Landon Cook.

The journey was challenging for our caravan. The roads were inconsistent in their patterns, which burdened our horses significantly. My colleagues and I had to continue our journey on foot as we passed the river and then to the mountain's root. As we rest, I can see the 'Cathedral of Vow' over the horizon: The twisted towers, long bridges, and round stone walls. It's a sight to behold... You have asked for my patience, but it is hard to contain myself when seeing this magnificent sight. I eagerly wait for the sun to rise once more—so we may venture inside and meet with the current residents.

-Phader Karthuras Rotolo.

1

There is some comfort to be had this morning. I and my colleagues awaken alongside our minor inconveniences, such as the soreness of our feet and the anticipation of the lugging of supplies. On the other hand, the cathedral brought this strange view of optimism. Its beauty secrets into our consciousness—though impractical the structure may seem. The architect must have studied the realms of fantasy to develop this abstract structure... We eat our morning meals before venturing as we rest by the warm fire; my colleagues talk briefly about the possibilities they might witness once they go inside. We all share the numerous tales and legends of what goes on inside and the purpose of this structure. I recall it fondly from my youth during the years of—'true freedom' in the capital; I am thankful that those times are over.

"Tell me, Karthuras," The knight with the black mustache asked for me, "Whatever happened to the previous Phader?"

I replied: "From what I could gather from his notes, he suffered from these troubling illusions, which led to his disappearance. There was no trail left behind in his wake, only doubt."

I might have spoiled their optimism; I hope that was not true. Admittedly, I'm concerned for my future. To be given the privilege at a young age to watch over the cathedral is a great honor and one I had faintly studied for. I can't imagine what the other Phaders think of me now. Then again—they are scattered far among the land of Erdphale.

Finally, we had prepared ourselves for the remaining miles left to wander. Once we climb over the hills, the 'Cathedral of vow' is only a hundred paces away. The loud bell alerts us of our arrival, and the echo disrupts the once-rested birds, scattering them in the opposite direction.

The large steel door opens to our presence, turned by the complex mechanical designs operated from within. In the dark shade, we could only hear the tapping of heels emitting louder with every step. Eventually, we see this stranger with a whole glance: The young woman greets us with a firm smile—perfecting her positioning and movement as if she were welcoming royalty. Her clothing is also impressive, with dark fabric and décor, yet there is beauty in the macabre.

She said: "You have arrived at last—Phader Karthuras Rotolo. We have been anticipating your arrival."

I replied: "And we are honored to have arrived at this place. May I ask your name?"

"My name is Cresalin. I am this Cathedral's caretaker, a mother of sorts some would consider. Though none share my blood, I am delighted to help those needing my assistance."

"By the designs of this structure, I can only imagine how—labyrinthine this place might be on the inside."

Her smile grew wider from my comment, "Not to worry, Phader. I shall escort you through the many hallways until you recognize every corner. For now, let us join inside."

Inside, we joined together to see the first of many rooms. Already, this place enchants me with its beauty. The pillars holding the structure are carved with depictions of malformed anatomies of the human form; Sleeper is at the ceiling, expanding his hands to make such creations. The cauldron also shares its signature design, with an eye in the middle wrapped in a bundle of hands and arms. The capital had similar artifacts—though lacking in creativity.

Few residents greeted themselves in our presence, humble in their poise and polite words. Among them, I encountered a few who had more obscure compositions. However, as human—as they seem at first glance, my curious eye could not ignore their disfigurement, such as the skin of their face flapping from every inch of movement. The eyes have a faint blue glow emitting from under the pupil. Do they have fake eyes? Not all had this same affliction, but one already begs my attention. That very attention had to be turned elsewhere as Cresalin led us to the next room where the food was prepared. This is where she stopped to offer us a meal and drink. Hastily, the others took upon the offer as I rejected it.

"Will you not join them?" She asked.

"My stomach is still satisfied from this morning..." I replied with a faint laugh.

"Then perhaps I can take you to your study instead."

"I would appreciate it immensely."

She leads me away from the others and again through the many halls. This time, the cauldron did not give us our much-needed light for guidance; instead, the sun's shine pressed through the azure glass windows. I turn my head to the cobblestone walls, finding the paintings intriguing. Their depictions are terrifying, and yet I find myself fond of them. Why am I drawn to this aesthetic? Cresalin is no different. Even now, the light brightens her pale face and the dark fabric she wears... it's becoming hard to focus on the path ahead.

She returns my curious glance with something to say: "I see you have curious eyes. Are the images to frightful?"

"They are abstract—but I find fascinating none of the less... They remind me of your uniform. The—darkness with a glamor of light, like a wandering lantern in the dead of night." Perhaps I was too bold to say such things to a stranger.

"Thank you for the compliment," she blushed, "few would ever consider such designs complimentary; not even the previous Phader found them amusing."

At that moment, I recalled a fragment of a letter from Phader that she had mentioned: '*Beasts with round eyes, lonely souls, and twisted minds. The eyes - the eyes see all! All that stands in those desolate halls and I who walk among the dark figures.*'

I decided to press the topic: "About the previous Phader, I had read many of his letters and found every entry to contain strange riddles. Did he ever come off as strange to you?"

"Yes..." she said with a concerned voice, "His mind became lost as his—eagerness to help people waned... It was a tragic day when he disappeared; many of us have felt his absence ever since. Sometimes we question if he's still around in spirit possibly."

"Spirit? You believe he's dead?"

"I don't see him returning anytime soon—the world outside our walls is unsafe."

"That is true. It took a group of well-armed knights to make it this far."

We walked up one of the many spiral staircases onto the second floor. The velvet carpet brightens the hallway, making it distinct from the rest. Following it forward, we ended up in one of the rooms. Cresalin gives me the key and allows me to open it... The room is modestly sized, with shelves containing many books. I opened one to find the historical records of one of the residents living in the cathedral.

"All of them contain everyone's family legacy," Cresalin confirmed, "You would be surprised to read their stories. Where they had started to where they are now."

"I can't imagine the countless tales everyone here has to share... Though, I prefer talking to people face to face. Perhaps you and I could spend time together and become more acquainted."

"I would much like to accept your offer if my current circumstances have not already been scheduled."

"I did not mean to intrude on your duties. Is there anything I can do to help?"

"Do not be alarmed, Phader. These matters require only my presence. But I won't hesitate to ask if I require your presence."

"Well—don't let me hold you from your responsibilities. I will return to the dining hall for supper. Will I meet you there?"

"Of course. I shall meet with you later." She walked out of the room with a slight nod.

Now, I am alone in this room, and with time, I have decided to investigate my surroundings for every tool and journal I can find. Figuring out the Phader may have left behind some notes or plans. None I was able to discover in these passing moments...

2

Garlic—oils—ale, and wheat, such a delightful sense; I follow its trail like a hook to a curious fish. I grew evermore famished from not having these delicacies in my gut. The trail led me to the dining hall, where everyone was gathered, delighting themselves with supper. I took part with a mug of ale in my right hand and a bowl of broth in my left. As I tried to enjoy these contents, the residents snuck in with warm gestures, leaving this food of mine to turn cold by the minute. This brightens my overwhelmed mind with a sense of wanting. Never in my early days did I ever feel truly wanted—this was a great contrast to me.

I wanted to speak to everyone, yet—I am focused on a single individual. I sought to find her amongst the crowed with no fragment of her being... Perhaps she was still attending to her matters.

Waiting for some time, I took the liberty to speak with the many residents in modest conversation. Slowly, the pattern of their dialogue became as clear as the cloudless sky. Though their years are older than mine—they speak like a child. Their voice had no ambition nor fear, only bliss and persistent delight. I had turned one of my simple questions into a counting game—to see how many times I would acquire the same answer. This question had to be simple to obtain a valuable response; I asked this: 'How do you feel when digging a six-foot hole?'

The answers are given using different words while preserving the same meaning: "I do not know how to use the stick of iron. It makes my hand sore, and my legs shiver.", "I—I had never touched such an object to know of its use. Such work is for the simple ones, is it not?" "I'm afraid I do not contain the strength to dig the soil in a timely matter."

With these answers, I contain only the foam of their thoughts; they seem somewhat capable of using the spoon and nothing more. With some extra time on my hands, I will further explore their thoughts.

As for my curious mind, wishes to see Cresalin once more before the night takes hold of our strength. I had taken one of the knights from my journey to accompany me in case of any danger. It took a moment to realize my guardian is not sober enough to walk presently in a straight-line, thus pressing himself against the wall for leverage.

A question occurred to me as of late. With that in mind, I ask: "What is your name?"

"M-my name...?" The knight said, wiping his black mustache, "It's Alen Deltoris... I would not be concerned with it—if I were you, Phader."

"Why do you say that?"

"I—not tend to stay here for long. By the morning, I will be heading back towards the capital."

"Does this place burden you already?"

"No... I have no intention of watching doors and—guiding hands to the shit bowls. I want to fight! To live!"

He trips over himself and then takes a moment to find his strength again. Before I could reply, a howl echoed from the spiral staircase. I promptly ran towards the upper platform, leaving Alen behind.

In the distance, I see Cresalin lying on the floor with bloodstained on her clothes. I ran over to check her current condition; there were only long claw marks on her belly, and no matter how many times I shook her, she would not allow her eyes to open... Turning to the dark room next to us, I saw red diamond-like eyes watching me with an increasing snarl rattling my ears.

"Evelyne..." Cresalin suddenly spoke out of breath, "Don't hurt him..."

This beast did not listen to her words and decided to pounce on me! Pinning me to the ground with her claws two inches from my eyes. I can hold her in place for the moment. Suddenly, she opens her jaw, protruding her long—rigid tongue against my cheeks. The sensation was like shards of glass grazing my skin. The more I try to resist her, the more persistent she becomes—damn it all, where is my help!? The minute I asked the question was the minute help came for me. Alen tackled the beast against her side, using his weight to keep her against the floor!

"Give me a hand with this beast!" He demanded from me.

"No, don't hurt her!" Cresalin cried out to Alen.

He ignored her plea, "Phader! Take the knife from my back pocket and slit this thing's throat!"

I hesitated the motion... even with her malformity. I could still see her human side.

"Phader!" Alen yelled for me once more.

Eventually, I removed myself from the floor and grabbed the knife from his sheath—I shivered with the blade pointed at the creature. My heart is pounding harder than I have ever experienced. I can hear Cresalin howling, begging me to let her go... My mind is being tugged back and forth! Eventually—I found my answer, which is why I am here at all... I demanded that Cresalin find me a rope or chain to keep this beast from attacking us. She follows my demand and returns to me with the bindings.

"What damn lunacy is this!" Alen growled, "Do you not see this beast? Are you blind? This thing was about to kill you, and now you intend to save her?"

She did not respond and began binding her friend while I helped Alen keep the creature at bay. When the knot was bound, she said, "Pull her into the room; we can keep her inside!"

It took some time to secure this creature. She lies on her bed, arms and legs bound to the steel frame. She twists and turns her limbs, trying to break free… And since I can look at this creature without much worry, I can concentrate on her features: This woman was corrupted by feline traits, meshing crudely with the human structure. The skin and fur were not well aligned, scattered, and torn as if she tried to scour her own flesh.

Alen asked: "What could have created this abomination?"

"She… She was not always like this," Cresalin explained, "Sleeper tends for her soul to be—transformed. For what…? I do not know."

Alen growled: "You're telling me Sleeper did this?"

"I… I don't know how else," she replied.

"Well, Phader?" Alen said sternly, "What do you make of this?"

I was short on words: "This is an unnatural occurrence."

"Pointless words, Phader… I need to kill this beast before she hurts anyone else."

"You will do no such thing!" Cresalin demanded, "Why would you murder an innocent life!?" she turned to me, "Are you not this realm's protector?"

"I think the three of us need some time to rest..." I said, rubbing my tired eyes, "As long as we keep Evelyne tied up in this room, we will have nothing to worry about."

Alen places his hand on his sword, "Do you expect me to rest tonight when this thing is still alive?"

I reply: "You will under my orders..."

Alen did not take my demand lightly. I could tell from his expression how much he wanted to strangle me. Before he could say or do anything else, he pushed himself away, leaving me and Cresalin alone with the beast.

"Thank you..." she said, walking closer to me, "I won't let this ever happen again. She—she is not always like this."

"You don't have to thank me. After all, the people who live under this roof, including Evelyne, are under my protective care. Tomorrow, you and I can arrange a way to properly secure her until we find a cure or a more suitable alternative."

She bowed her head while giving me the most genuine smile I had ever seen on a woman. For a moment, I forgot everything that had happened to me so far.

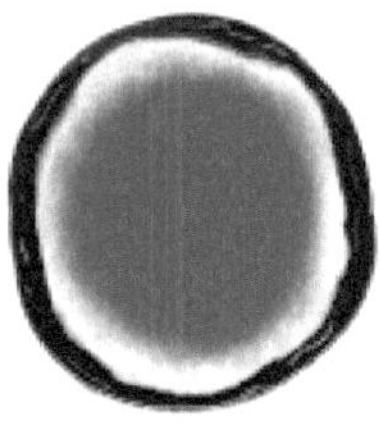

Everyone returned to their chambers as Evelyne's wailing never ceased. Constant cacophony to my ears, turning the simple pleasure of rest into a luxury—damn it all, why would Sleeper create such a strange beast? It's difficult for me to plan a tolerable way to care for her... The cries radiate louder with every passing moment. Even in my blissful moments of vision, it's soon abrupt.

The silence finally came when I did not expect it to arrive. My ears can take a moment of rest... And yet, my mind is not diminished from this worry. This night will never cease at this rate; to cure this burden, I throw on my mantle, ignite my lantern, and then venture towards Evelyne's bed chamber again...

I notice the open door to Evelyne's room when traveling through many hallways, turning, and ascending the staircase. The thumping of my heart drums again as my back streams a cold sensation... how poised I am in this desolate hall; the rational side beckons me to turn away. Persistent that fear was... even so, I must take responsibility and know if she escaped her bindings.

Venturing inside, I could only see the empty bed, stained in blood, that trails towards the window frame. I investigate further, seeing the creature standing on the lower rooftops... she basks—in the moon's glow with her back arched and eyes sealed. When she turned her gaze to me, I had to question the realm of my sanity. The woman beast before me danced in the light as she moaned with her songful voice. Licking her fingers, she then touches herself while using her free hand to beckon me over... I had never seen such a sight in my life. Ghastly poses of lustful temptations, a coaction of alchemy that should never be tested—yet I must confess my strange fascination. Like a painting, I could never remove from my sight...

Still, she beckons me, hoping I will commit to the peril. I must remove myself from this place! To the halls, I fled then to the room where I lay secluded... The undying fire eats away my heart from that fear. Perhaps this was just a dream, an illusion plaguing my mind from the lack of rest. It has been a long journey, and the stress of being the cathedral's protector drags me to the void of unease.

My body spirals from this madness; I grasp onto my surroundings to hold myself in place—away from temptation. Before I knew it, I stood in the middle of my room... Staring into the darkness, I see that damn silhouette from before. Evelyne is in my room, watching me shiver with her vertical eyes.

She presses herself against the wall, limbs stretched, and mouth open to me. She moans with a slight purr as her tail protrudes at me. My mind drowns in euphoria... Thus, I took a step closer and went on many steps until my hands reached for her neck. This—wasn't for my defense; no, an urge pulses through my body to commit this corrupted motion.

She doesn't detract from my advance... she takes it willingly, moaning with ecstasy. The sharp tongue protrudes from her lips, waiting in anticipation.

I... I no longer care for anything else in this world. We will not be dissatisfied.

'dissatisfied' are the words uttered in my mind once I open my eyes to the cobblestone wall. I stand alone, with cold, numbed legs from the prolonged use. Dawn revealed its light to me; the morning had already begun.

"Are you awake, Phader?" Cresalin asks behind the door.

I took a deep breath and turned myself over at the door. Cresalin is standing before me—still, she has that pleasant smile.

"Have you thought more about Evelyne?" she asked.

"I... Sorry, I was not able to think properly last night. This head of mine was eating the thoughts I gave it," I laughed nervously.

"With some oats in that belly, I'm sure your mind will focus again!"

"Let us hope... Before we do, I should put on some modest clothing."

"Oh-yes! Of course," her face turns slightly red as she steps back, pushing herself away from my sight.

I should probably prepare myself before they become eager to relieve me from this solitude...

When I had partaken in my meal with everyone else, a foul aura surrounded my mind in anticipation. I knew Evelyne would not be in the best condition—far from it. I should say that my dream or experience was more than just an illusion. This may be conflicting to me to some extent... The three of us eventually gathered: Cresalin, Alen, and I. We took many steps to reach our destination, filled with bitter silence. Alen's stern manner kept his hand firmly on the sword's handle, desperate he was to slay this beast. Once we reached the door frame leading into her room, our silence turned to awe... Evelyn is nowhere to be seen. The two venture inside, investigating their surroundings while I stand here helpless. The evidence of my act of murder is gone from my grasp. Where exactly? My room is clean and well-organized. I also had a check under the bed;

my knowledge of this cathedral is only a crooked brush along the dusty surface. I would not have known where to place the body—nor what I had committed such a crime to begin with.

Cresalin holds herself by grasping onto her shoulders, "Evelyne... Where are you?"

"That damn beast is loose!" Alen growled as he turned to me, "You've endangered everyone here!"

I replied: "It's possible... I must admit to my unthoughtful actions; I try to care for everyone at once—and now I must pay for my choices."

"You did what's right!" Cresalin said confidently, even though I was still unsure of my actions.

"Great..." Alen huffed, "I have dealt with a beast and a boy leader. My-my does Sleeper like to jest with me."

"Sleeper enjoys toiling with us, which I can agree on. But what matters now is everyone's safety. Alen, I know you want to leave this place. These circumstances are too great to ignore, but you must agree to stay here if the worst happens to us all."

Cresalin scoffed, "Why would we keep this oaf? He does not care for any soul but his."

"My soul is worth keeping—I must ensure everyone is safe from the evils lurking around every corner... When you need someone to slay bandits, I am the one who comes to your beck and call." He left the room before any more words were said against him.

"Phader..." Cresalin asked for me, "You must help me find Eveyln before something bad happens to her or anyone else."

"I will do what I can for her...You have my word as a man, a Phader, and a friend."

3

Seven days have not passed since the night of Evelyn's death. During that time, I acquainted myself with the many residents and spent many hours searching for evidence. For a first impression, I had already left a curious imprint that made others nervous about my presence. There have been no foul words or toil in my days, but you never know what might come the following week.

Wandering through this long hall, I come across an old man who stumbles as he carries the many books within his breast, struggling with the chance of tripping over himself; before such trials occurred, I took the liberty to offer him my assistance.

I said: "Excuse me, sir, you seem burdened by the weight of books in your hand. May I offer you my own?"

He presses himself against the stone wall and takes a short breath to gain back his strength, "You—think me useless, you damn brat!? I have you know I can lift swords heavier than you."

"I do not doubt your capabilities, my friend, but you seemed overwhelmed. It is my duty as a Phader to help those in need."

"A Phader, you say…? The man who speaks the words of our god and spits his intuition on the many. Tell me, boy, what does Sleeper say to a shite like you?"

"I only question his words and use the meanings for the good of the people. I'm sure Sleeper would fancy himself a bottle of wine than speak to me."

"Is that so?" he grunted from the burden of taking over his strength. Before the books fell, I had taken half of his stack. When given slight relief, he scoffs at me: "Duty to help those in need, aye...? If you were not Sleeper's servant, would you still help me?"

"I would like to think so."

He did not utter another word to me and decided to continue down his path. The silence was bitter, and my good nature followed its resolve... I remember being asked, 'Why would you help those who are foul to you?' The answer to me had always been simple, man or woman—we had all dealt with our strife daily, bliss being a rare luxury. If you give a helping hand to those in need, they shall walk with a smile now or later that night. Being a Phader has pushed this idea to me, but I genuinely believe in helping others... even if I had to question myself as of late.

We left the final step of the spiral staircase and went to the lower halls, where the old man led me to the library... A library indeed, the collection is more extensive than anticipated. My curious glance skimmed the many book titles.

"Well... Are you going to laugh at the old man who reads the books of our world?"

"The titles of these novels are curious..."

The books are history and Philosophy, based on old beliefs and stigmas. Even the ones that describe utter hatred towards the Phaders. The old man continued: "Old and curious they are, a youngling such as yourself will never understand the thoughts of the wise... And—as your elder, I say that you are a fraud underneath that black cloak; the gold ropes on your shoulder are weaved with lies and deceit. Sleeper is not real, nor are your beliefs!"

"You may think of me as a deceitful troubadour, which is far from the truth. If I could give you my inner thoughts..."

"You can't show me anything!" he interrupted, "Don't waste my time with words of the weak... this is no place for such nonsense."

"Then you and I have nothing more to say..." I said, defeated.

"Yes! A triumph moment indeed..."

I left his sight, returning to the corridor. I became lost in my thoughts, wondering why someone pushed me away like so. Then again, the callous circumstance will hamper one's ability to socialize politely.

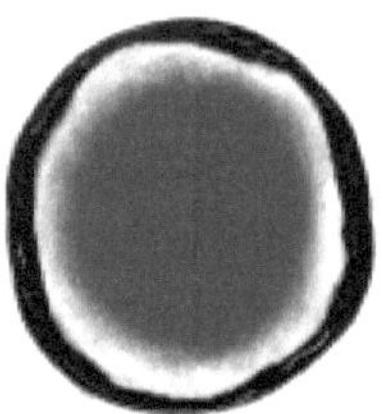

A few hours turn as the sun sets aside Sleeper's ring. To pass this flowing river of time, I take a moment to join Cresalin in conversation. We joined together in my study where we sat on opposite ends, taking moments of respite—by sipping the mugs of ale... Unfortunately, it is a bit light on flavor.

"Tell me, Cresalin," I asked, "How does someone such as yourself find yourself under the cloak of Sleeper?"

"Do you object to my duties?" She said, worried.

"Not at all," I reassured, "You would make a great candidate for the Cathedral's advisor. I find it strange how I was selected for this role. Is your presence not known to the Capital?"

"I have no motivation to convince of my worthiness, for the people here see me as their mother—the guiding hand for the lost."

"And you not burdened by this?"

"I have no reason to be. I had grown alongside them, knowing almost everything about them."

"Come now, you can be honest with me. Caring for the many will weigh the mind greater than any armor on a knight."

"I suppose there is some worry... Like Evelyne, for instance. Have you found any new information about her?"

My expression seeps despair, "I'm afraid to say that—I have not learned anything new. I took some time out of my day to follow any trail I could, yet there was nothing I could find."

"It's a shame... And Phader, forgive me for placing this burden on you."

I waved my hand, "I take full responsibility..."

She takes a sip of her ale while hiding her worried expression. Glancing away momentarily, I tried to think of another topic of interest. Think away as I did; she has already set course among the populace. She thanked me for my company and left my study. Taking the time, I needed to set aside the pitcher and mugs. Looking outside the window, I find the old man from before sitting on the bench below me. Weird this position is to the common eye; I turn away before anyone thinks my curious gaze was that of stalking... Then again, the words he said to himself were—fascinating. Mumbling in isolation, bitter words in tone: "How can our community be corrupted by greed and speak of gods and philosophy with the simple mind! The people should be free and not worrying over petty tribulations…"

I somewhat agreed with his monologue—knowing that most people think collectively. Their worries over simple matters become a heavy burden when everything becomes an easy chore.

He continued: "I know the truth, far greater than any man or woman…! Damnit… Why was I burdened with this knowledge? Was I supposed to be a martyr? Yes! Yes! I shall shape their minds like I, and we no longer fear these worrisome trials in the capital."

My accord turns to suspicion; this old man locks himself within the cage of his mind and expects to change the world in the blink of an eye. Having passed his youth, what does he hope to accomplish? And… What does he mean by the worrisome trials in the capital? When I had left my home, there were minor disputes, but none befitting a revolt or organization of chaos.

He took a deep breath and spoke to someone I could not see, "Show me the visions 'All Seeing Eye,' let me learn of these trials so I may learn from them."

'Is he mad?' I wondered.

From that point forward, he remains in silence. Allowing his thoughts—his person to turn colder by the minute. Lost forever in his mind.

I turned away from the sorry sight, then stretched my fingers against the dusty shelves. Though I do not know his name, I am tempted by his past. I want to learn what turns his cold heart. No… I should not scavenge for simple text; rather, I should speak to him further if I can manage it. Difficult it may be, and yet I strive for the mile more.

I had walked that mile to find him alone in that same spot. He stares continually at the grass below his shoes, never blinking his eyes.

I suddenly speak to grab his attention: "May I accompany you?"

The dots in his eyes dilated from my interference, and his focus centered on me, "Your very presence is a nuisance, boy. Why would I want your company?"

"Being alone with your thoughts can hinder your outlook on life. Would you not agree?" "Don't be foolish—the mind must be focused, Vigilant! When times of great disorder come, I must keep this head soaked in the waters of knowledge. Do you not see the corruption and disorder?"

"There are weeds in the garden, yes, but it is not my place nor in my power to change the world in my image... Let alone change many souls. You should focus on your surroundings for a change."

"Oh yes! I should stare at the many empty halls and listen to the children babble on and on about how much this day bores their simple minds."

Frustrated, I sighed, "What led you to this sorry state?"

He took a moment to respond, "People, they are unpredictable and callous..."

"Now, I must ask. Where are you getting this information from? We're far from the capital, and messengers rarely visit such places."

Suddenly, he became nervous, grasped his knee, and looked away, "Why are you leeching onto me? You must enjoy watching your elders turn to ash."

"Nonsense... I am here because you left a curious print on my mind. A print I must discover for myself. I know you are talking to someone who I cannot see... Tell me, is this entity a demon or Phantom?"

He clenched his teeth, shaking his head with the widest grin I had ever seen on a man, "Sleeper's mouthpiece once to know the truth of it all! You could not comprehend such sights... Better to live in ignorance, I say."

"Live in ignorance... Are you expressing your thoughts? Well—I shall not waste your time anymore, but if you want to accompany me for a drink, you are more than welcome to join."

"One day, boy. You will see how bitter this world truly is."

"I know the mind far more than I let on, and yet—I walk the mile more."

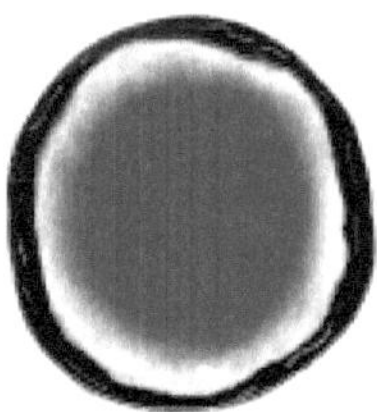

The mile more, I ventured through the cathedral, finding solace among the dark, vacant rooms that spread throughout this place. It is incredible to see vast space without occupants wandering, let alone discussing pointless topics. No, what remains now is old furniture, cobwebs, and dust. The more I strayed, the darker this place became. Eventually, I had to stop myself and turn back to my studies.

From there, I took a moment to rest my limbs and listen to the hollow ambiance. Such music was abrupted before I was able to enjoy its calm melody... I can hear a voice beckoning me. The room darkens into this strange black shade. I tried to escape from this room but became lost in the void with no door in sight.

The sun reveals only a part of itself before me. From there—I could see something. The light shows me a blackened statue perched in the way of wonderment. The statue stands alone in the darkened void. I walk closer, and not soon after, I see the stone chips falling from—flesh? Red, pulsing lively to my presence.

A great breath exhales from his lips, exposing his bare teeth and bright violet eyes, staring with a wide, unblinking gaze.

"Let me show you the world..." the statue said with a—almost human-like voice.

"Show me the world? Could I not gaze at it with my own eyes?"

"You only see the world that surrounds you... Do you want to see all of it? The wars—the beautiful woman and the fate of this world?"

"There is no need for me to gaze into oblivion. Should I not be content with my condition?"

"Only if you want to live your life unknowing of its fate. Allow me to show you..."

"I do not need such sights. To be burdened with truth will only lead me into the pitiful spiral."

The statue chuckled, "You will allow yourself the path of ignorance?"

"I would better for me to live unknowingly..."

"Why would you betray your intellect!?" The old man appears from the darkness, standing beside the statue while grasping the black stone arm. "There must be something you wish to know that has been bothering you since your arrival?"

The truth about Evelyn's disappearance. That question burdens my mind, but I must retract from viewing the stranger's perspective.

"There is something, isn't there?" The old man continued.

"Everyone wishes to have their questions answered, but I must reframe myself—for I may give in to the lonely spiral... I hoped that my words could convince you to remove yourself from comfort and experience the world through a different lens, and yet—It's too late for you to change."

"You're a fool, youngling..."

"I am a student learning the world outside the many books."

The black stones that crumbled off the statue began resting on the flesh... watching as this black cloud evaporated from my surroundings. Pressing myself against my desk, I take a moment to catch my breath. The sense of relief is absent, replaced with weariness... There is some vitality left in this body of mine, and with its last drops, I should check on that old man again. When I arrived at his chambers, the door was already wide. A foul smell creeps into my nostrils. Upon my investigation—the smell could not counter the sight before me. A mutant of disfigured proportions. I stare at a creature whose head contains a black void, and his forehead limbs lack structure.

Expressing only regret, the old man looks at me with discontent... My dread planted me like a tree. I could never turn myself away from that sight.

He muttered words that I could not understand. However, the black void in his head spoke more to me than I had previously encountered... A spiral of calamity, depictions of abstract images, resembling... I constrained myself to look at those images any further. Now focused on the old man again, I see the blood trickling down from his eyes and ears. The pain must be too much to bear, and with the limited time I have, there is nothing I can do to end his suffering... No, there is something. Committing to this motion of mine, I would have to ask myself, 'Is it justified?' Contemplating will get me nowhere; his moaning grows louder by the passing minute... I see a dagger next to his mutilated hand. I retrieved it and then aimed the edge against the lump of his neck.

I—try to convince myself that there is another way to save him. Yet, I must remind myself that I am no god—no martyr, just a man who chose to take these burdens for himself. There is no pleasure, no growth in my reputation, and my obligations as a Phader play no part.

With this final moment, I tell him, "There will be peace in the land of dreams. May you finally rest there."

"There—will... be nothing more me... Just the void," The old man uttered his final words, and now—I stand alone with a blade coated with his blood...

How bitter this was for me to participate in... foolish the old man was. He did not deserve such torment. There is nothing more I could do for him besides prepare his body and hope he arrives in the next world.

4

I stood before my people on the podium, speaking the many words I had written down the previous night. The light shines upon them with Sleeper's image looming over, standing, and watching our lord look on in wonderment, or so the glass panels depict. The lecture was far from perfect... Once I said my words of prayer, I opened the confession booth to anyone in desperate need. Alone for hours, the comfort of my chair is getting the better of me, and now I wish to rest for a long while. The muttering outside these walls gave me a great ambiance in which to drift easily from reality... A loud creak that awakened me to the stranger's presence. I turn my eyes over to the shadow behind the translucent curtain. I cannot see their faces, let alone ask for their names. My position forbids me from doing so. After all, people speak of their ills once they are free from the wondering eyes.

"Phader—oh Phader, will you hear my confession?" She spoke passionately.

I replied: "Speak of your ill words so your mind can finally rest."

"There is a phantom inside of me... Callous as the dull knife. Day by day, a temptation stirs my heart to the foulest. I can hear the voice in my head. My body moves and twitches of its own accord. Even now, it lingers on."

Like a riddle, I must answer these confessions accordingly: "Temptations will always stir the soul when agitated by something present in our lives. What could cause these problems of yours?"

Her slender fingers poke through the steel grate as she tries to push away my curtain, "A certain man, the one who roams the many halls and listens to the many minds. A stranger I wish to see more... Phader, will you allow yourself to see me at my worst?"

I was lost for words at that instant.

She presses her chest against the iron bars, expecting me to unveil the curtain. I had to resist such a temptation by leaving this booth, but the door would not open.

"Phader..." She said, "I know you are not allowed to see the faces of those on the other side. Allow me to cover so you may honor the code."

"I don't want this!"

The curtain slides away by an unknown force, revealing the woman on the other side. True to her word, the face is covered with a black fabric with a decorative ring around her face. As for the rest of her body, she wore nothing else. Naked and wanting, she expects me to fulfill her whims and ease her suffering... I must confess that my arousal is shifting my thoughts; the desire is for not, for there is no way for me to enter the other side. I had to control these urges. This lunacy is a profound burden; how can I live in this state of being?

She begins moving her body intensely, expressing her wanting, uttering the words 'take me!' repeatedly. My body boils within with this anger, this—need to satisfy... She offers herself to me. Would it be wrong of me to not—take...

My hands brush past those iron bars, gripping the twins on her chest! She moans like a desperate whore wanting more of me! Not to worry... For I to need my fill of pleasure. My fingers unveiled a fragment of her round face, showing me the lips masked with black lipstick. Penetrating through the gap, I taste her from the inside—those soft moans vibrate our tongues while they spring in repetition. Oh, how I wanted to take her here and now, but this damn booth constrains me within this permanent state of torment! She suddenly pushes me away. What is this?

"Do not fret, Phader, my love. You shall have every piece of me in time."

I became out of breath, hot as the fiery coals. I take a moment to sit down, eventually easing my pain... Those thoughts of mine, did I lose control of myself? Vulgar, my intentions were at that moment. I cannot comprehend the idea. This isn't me... I must help those in need, not fulfill my devious fantasies... What—happened to me?

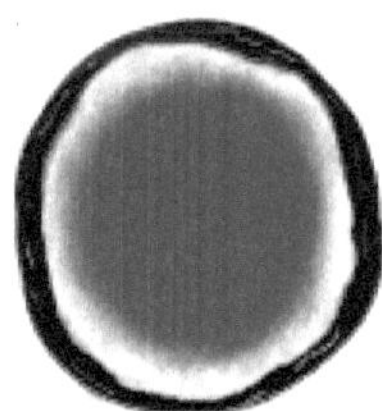

That same night, I entered my bed chambers, wanting to break this pain away. I had a few strong drinks to calm my mind from any more temptations that came my way. What a jest that motion was when committed. The longing still consumes my body beyond what I can control... I'm accompanied by those sights that fade in. I hold myself, twisting and turning—wishing for this pain to go away. When opening my eyes, this damn reality of mine taunts me with feminine physic! Limbs protruded out among the walls, legs—arms, and lips appeared. When I close my eyes, the alluring musk takes hold of me—as the mind acts with purpose of desire...

The maiden is calling for me in desperation. I could not bear to see such soft skin wither without the touch of my hand... She is playful, spawning from the wall only to retract once I'm close enough to catch those—elegant shapes.

"Do you love me...?" she allures.

"Desires of love are a game, my dear," I laughed, "Would you not prefer the desires of the flesh at this moment? You must be longing to partake in such delights!"

She did not respond to my words of bastard wisdom. She only lets on with her poses that disappear and reappear instantly.

I yelled: "How long will you make me wait!? Were you not eager to have me before!?"

Again, this harlot did not respond. My patience grows thin as my desires devour my own body. Such hunger is ravenous! Why must she torment me so? Does she not want me? This—head of mine is twisting the very innards I hold behind this drapery of flesh! I... I...

I attempt to refrain my tongue from begging for short-term delights. After all, it will never satisfy the cravings—only growing their desires further obscure... This isolation is too much for one to handle.

Closing my eyes, I try to rest under these stressful conditions. The liquor did not hamper the eager part of me—only at least, spinning the world at nausea until I fell into that deep drunken slumber.

5

The sky's mysterious curtain shades my world to an auburn crimson. I stand with Cresalin outside the cathedral's walls to the scattered farmlands. The smell of manure is abundant, yet the clear view interweaves me. The trees are miles away as the mountains subside in the background. How fortunate I am to spend this beautiful night with her company... This was nothing more than a formality, of course. She offered a detailed tour inside and outside the cathedral's walls. However, I needed a break from the sight of my predicament...

The old man had been buried the day prior with a—lacking attendance. It was unfortunate. I hope his next life will be more pleasant wherever he goes... Then, there was that experience I had with the apparition. The strange sights were one of many concerns I had that night. My—inner self leashes my actions and words, thus portraying me as a deviant... What stirred within me to become that man? Perhaps my dedication to my profession has left me in an isolated state—or the nature of my being sought revenge.

I suddenly wonder if Cresalin has ever had this problem before, of course I would never ask such questions. But there was a question I did have: "I had never thought the community would be this well-organized. Were you not amply supplied by the capital?"

Cresalin adjusted her hands over her lower abdomen before she spoke, "We were never sure that your people could keep us satisfied forever. Surely, it would be beneficial to prepare."

"It was a wise decision…" I glance at the fields, "How many farmers do you have out there?"

"Just the two families, The Grestavs and the Howlis. The families usually visit the chapel once a week. Most of the time, they spend their days in the fields."

"What about that hooded stranger over there?" I pointed in the direction.

Cresalin notices the garments of this character. The hood was rounded, just like hers, but the color was a different shade, violet instead of black. The gold strands are out on the back instead of the shoulders.

"I do not know of him…" she replied.

"Phader!" a man called out for me. He runs towards me, panting and distressed.

I patiently wait for his response.

"Derek Grestav be the name, sir," he said with a slight bow, "I did not come to you for a simple chat. My daughter needs your help!"

I replied with a short response: "Lead me."

Together, the three of us rushed across the fields until we reached Derek's house. Inside, he led us to one of the closed rooms where his wife stood distraught in front of the door.

He said to her: "Tis alright, my love. Cresalin and the preacher are here to help our daughter." He carefully leads us away from the door and then nods to go in.

I open the door with Cresalin behind me; together, we witness a young girl entangled in a dreary circumstance. Pale as snow, eyes darkened from the lack of rest. Compared to a corpse, there would be a minimal difference.

Cresalin walks forward to meet with Youngling. Lowering herself with a reassured smile, she then asks for the girl's name. No reply was given. She tries again with a different question: "Did somebody hurt you?" Still, no reply has been given.

Derek explains the details: "Some entity has possessed my daughter, Isabella. Her mind is not like it used to be."

Cresalin confidently said: "The Phader and I can solve any problem. I can assure you..."

I asked Derek if he could explain the recent events that could lead to this issue. Everything seemed normal except for The scarecrow he mentioned; his daughter has a strange fascination with the object. Her father caught her talking and—feeding it her scraps as well. Going as far as to watch it happen during the night, then stabbing it with his knife. In time, he is convinced of a rodent and nothing more... And even if it was a rodent, it should be properly disposed of.

Cresalin and I set out to perform such a task.

She asked me: "Do you expect there to be something strange about this object?"

"Everything that has happened to me in the past month has been strange... This is no different. From what I have learned, the supernatural is unpredictable—inconsistent in devious ways."

I examined the entire scarecrow until noticing the torn hole at the back. At first, I figured the farmer stuffed straw inside without patching the hole. That idea was tossed once I noticed the piece of ripped fabric near my boot. It had been sealed before... No rodent would carefully remove the patch in a precise manner.

I grab the scarecrow's shoulder, then shake it violently to see if anything moves inside. There is not a single stir or sound to be heard from. This entity is patient... Like the confident idiot, I plunge my left hand into the bundle of straw to find anything unusual... I felt a moist object. I pulled it out and saw a long tan root. Continuing with the same strand led me to the end or beginning rather. It was a large potato; the texture was rough and muddy as if it had been dragged across the field multiple times. The shape is uncanny, resembling a warped face. It did not take a minute to wonder if this was the anomaly.

I return with the spud firmly grasped around my fingers. I said to Derek: "Warm your fire. I have the rodent you seek."

"Rodent...? Are you jesting, preacher?" he scoffed.

"Warm the fire—and we will find out."

He kindles the dry wood pieces without any more questions until the flames scorch the lumber.

Indeed, a potato does not easily get engulfed in the flames and rather softens the contents within. At best, the skin will char... I want evidence of his spud being a living entity with its own concealed thoughts. The fire will make it talk or scream in agony. Without delay, I tossed the potato into the fire—only for it to catch me within its roots! The damn thing penetrated my skin and swung around! I let out a faint grunt as I tried to remove it. The others quickly rush over to assist me! Cresalin grabs the potato, trying to jerk the roots out of my skin. Suddenly, the shape opens, revealing human-like eyes and mouth-containing teeth.

Derek rushes over with a hatchet, ready to tear it apart. The plant hastily removes itself from my limbs and squirms out the door before the hatchet blade can reach it. We kept chasing this bastard through the crop field to the forest and, eventually, the cave. We had to stop our trail here.

I told the others: "It's too dangerous to go inside. We should gather some men and supplies."

"Phader, we must do something about that thing!" Derek insisted.

"I shall remain here and keep watch. Just in case he tries to escape."

"Your arm!" Cresalin pointed out, worried.

I raised my arm, seeing the blood trickling down and around my hair fibers. "It has a slight burning sensation and nothing more. I will be fine for now."

"Here, Phader," Derek said while holding the hatchet, "You should at least be armed when fighting that beast."

I took it and replied with a simple nod... Before I knew it, I was alone in the wilderness, waiting for this creature to reveal itself as the others gathered hastily.

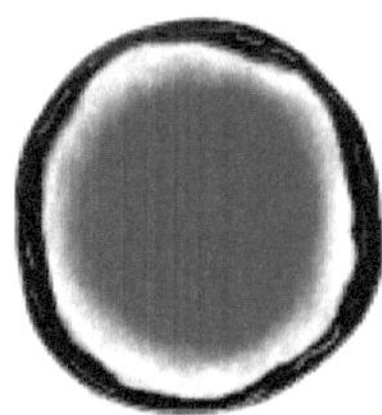

That Auburn sky dissipates into a nightly curtain. My only light source came from the crackling flames of the makeshift fire. I rest by its side, keeping my eyes peeled towards the abyss. With the hatchet in my grasp, I felt slightly unease from this whole predicament—though anxious about the outcome. Just as my fears start creeping into this dear ole head of mine.

Cresalin and a group of knights come to my side, armed and ready for the task.

She spoke first: "I had brought the aide you requested, Phader."

Alen scoffed, "I see you finally have taken my advice. Killing these damn creatures is truly the best and only option."

I replied: "There is no time to quarrel over previous matters. I expect you to get the job done and nothing more."

He said nothing more.

I turned to Cresalin, "You should stay out here with someone by your side. I do not know what lies beyond that void."

"I'm coming with you, Phader," she said, gripping my hand, "Please, we are in this together!"

I only wanted to keep her safe from any danger... but her eagerness could not be ignored, and it might be more dangerous out here than inside; alas, only time will tell. "Stay close to me..." I replied, then turned to the other knights, "Let's go inside and rid the world of this foul creature."

There was nothing more unsavory than venturing into the depths. Surrounded by the endless dark, the sun's warming beams will never permit entry here. Just the light I and my colleagues have in hand. The deeper we transversed, the question of quantity brought forth an extra layer of worry. Perhaps that's my paranoia kicking me... That smell, rancid that damn smell was when it entered my senses. Earthly yet—rotted with a glaze of copper. My surroundings became humid, reflecting our forms among the abstract stones. I turn over to Cresalin for a moment. Her face gave no fearful expression but rather a familiar look. She turns her head to the side, expecting a shaped stone to be present. She then turned her gaze towards me as I looked away.

My curious nature did not permit me to watch my step. Stained on my boot, I find a strange black substance drooling with a white slime. That smell, this rot, I now know what this is. It might seem like a joke, but someone could be stashing spuds here.

A figure emerges from the darkness suddenly, then walks forward into the light of my torch. The round hood with clothes dyed violet instead of black. There was something strange about his eyes. They were grey as the clouds in the sky; the pupils turned in every direction without much focus.

The knights readied their swords as they took to my side. To calm tensions, I speak to the stranger: "Greetings, I am a Phader to the 'Cathedral of Vow.' We have come for a beast lurking down here."

"I know not of this beast..." he replied coldly, "It would be wise for you all to turn back now."

"Why so?" I replied.

"Can't you see he's hiding something!" Alen blurted out.

"I hide nothing of value, stranger," he readjusts his round hood. "This place is dark for the mind to handle. Staying for too long could produce troubling outcomes... The presence of phantoms. They are not meant to be seen for too long; they require the naked eye."

"We are not planning to stay here for long..." I reassured him, "We are hunting for only one thing. Once we have it—you will no longer have to worry about us anymore."

"You speak words of peace, Phader. A counter to that of your god... What are you doing, dwindling yourself in that old religion? Do you expect me to trust you?"

"I do not know what you mean. I speak to you as a friend and nothing more—nor less."

"Spoken like the trickster god, 'Blood,'" he scoffed.

"We are wasting time here," Alen rushed. He gripped the stranger's hood and tugged him closer, "You will step out of the way before I break every bone in your body."

The stranger's gaze did not show fear nor hatred, only patience.

Alen tosses him and waves for the others to follow.

"I apologize for my friend," I said to the stranger.

He remains still against the wall as I and the others continue forward. It did not take long for us to reach the cavern's end. The walls are covered with that same black and white substance, oozing onto the surface. There are hills scattered around, containing only potatoes in every stack. The stench finally reached its peak, leading Cresalin to almost vomit from its musk.

"How are we supposed to find this bastard!?" Alen said in his frustration.

"Do not fret," I said, "It is very different than the common you see before you. The roots of this creature act like its limbs. These do not contain the roots they once possessed, giving us an advantage."

Everyone was silent as they examined the piles. Not knowing how long this search would take, they thought of retreating. Remembering the oath to their community, they eventually gave in to their—uncomfortable surroundings.

Minutes have passed since we began. In our time, there was no progress to be made, or so it seems now. My findings lead me to find something of interest. Upon the blood-stained bedroll, a red book lays on the pillow. I took it and then concisely read its contents. These pages contain personal entries from a man named Sarian. For now, I closed the book and kept it under my arm.

"I'm finding nothing here..." said Alen, "It may have returned outside—and that stranger could be a danger to us. What should we do with him?"

I approached the man again, "Sarian, it is dangerous for you to stay here. Please come with us."

"My name is not—Sarian..." the stranger replied, "I am the Galik-Brusadore. The one who speaks for the goddess of autonomy."

"Galik-Brusadore?" I questioned, "I have heard of that title somewhere before, but I do not kno—" my memories strike like a hammer; I recall his kind, his religion... "How many of you are there?"

"Only I..."

This bastard is lying to me, "Alen, take Galik to the dungeon. I can't have his kind roaming these lands."

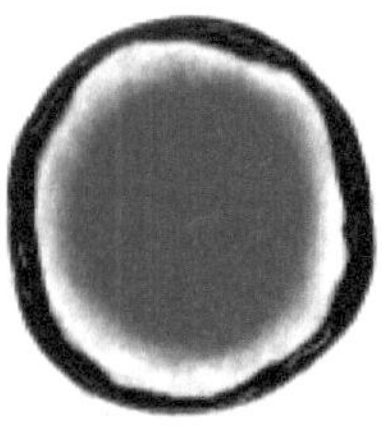

My patience can only last so long until I make an aggressive decision. Yet, when I had the Galik locked away in the cathedral, I knew it was the right one to make. True, he had not committed any crimes as far I know, but his religion (which follows the teachings of Hettalies) has done more devious deeds than the common bandit; no, they are bandits... Before I became a Phader, the capital was in ruin because of their beliefs. I can still remember those days with a sour feeling in my stomach... However, with these thoughts in my head, I must focus on what is most important.

The moon hangs over the horizon as the final hours play their lasting Symphony. I rest at the table alongside Cresalin and one of the many knights. We keep the family's house on guard in case the creature makes its return. Passing the time, I opened the book I had previously taken and then began reading its—uncomfortable tales, richly diseased with an obsession hidden behind the words of pietism.

Sleeper has blessed me with the soul of purity—away from all corruption. A longing tears my soul as she roams the fields, guiding her hands along the flowing waters. I shall take her for myself—so no one can intrude upon the simple mind...

I was appalled by his reference to Isabella. The final page struck me more than before—an occurrence none would dare consider. The page includes an image of the creature I had encountered before, along with the body of a man bleeding onto it.

My dearest Isabella. The Galik Brusadore has offered me something I cannot refuse—a chance for you and me to live forever in eternity. The process is a painful one... But the sanctity of our love is eternal! My blood will spill upon the soil, sprouting a form that can live off the very essence of this world.

"Did you find anything interesting?" Cresalin suddenly asked me.

"I found pages that describe one's obsession... I have never seen anything in my life that contains such wickedness."

"Then why do you keep it with you? Would it be better to destroy it?"

"I must keep it for evidence—and though I'm skimming through the pages, I find many interesting pieces of information. For example, the concept of soul transference, the bending of reality through living beings..."

"You find the rituals of Hettalies interesting? I never thought you would consider the idea."

"I don't consider them for practice—no, I might find the scattered information useful to my understanding of these rituals..."

Before I spoke anymore, I had to remind myself that speaking of any interest in the Demoness Hettalies could send me to a swift execution. After all, she is a taboo because of her involvement in the downfall of our kingdom. Witnessing such tragedies rots me from the inside, remembering those days—again, I digress from the topic.

I continued: "Sarian obsession is clearly stated in his words. He will stop at nothing until he takes Isabella for himself."

"What do you propose?"

I replied: "Waiting here for one night will do nothing for us in the long-term... Stupidity might flow through my thoughts when I say this, but I—should provoke him."

She slightly chuckled, "Truly, you can't be serious, Phader."

"We could hunt him down in the forest for days, but we would be wasting our time doing so. It would be beneficial to end the parasite now." I turned to the knight, "What do you say? Will you help me find him?"

The knight did not respond to my question, nor could I see any expression under his steel helm. He leans forward on the table, pressing his palms against the surface, grunting in agony. "No—need..." The knight grunted, "I'm already here!"

The knight unsheathes his sword and then stumbles at me, twirling the blade sporadically! I jumped out of the way in time, leaving the knight to trip over himself. "This—body is useless!" He groaned. Underneath the fabric, I noticed something crawl towards the gap, leaving a puddle of blood in his wake.

The spud reveals itself to me with a stern glare, eyes pulsating with teeth bared and ready to bite. "Why must you quarrel in my affairs, preacher!?"

I replied: "Your obsession is harming the people around you! Look at yourself now—your current state, how can one go so far?"

He crawls away from my sight, "There is no need for your words, preacher. You can rot in oblivion!"

I ran over to the fallen knight, retrieving the blade from his dead hand. Meanwhile, I hear Derek and Cresalin calling for help as they try to catch the freak... Once I could pry out the handle, I turned around instantly, charging the next. I find Derek wounded with holes through his legs while Cresalin and Isabella are in the same room together. The creature leaps onto the little girl, attaching the roots against her flesh. Cresalin attempts to pull him off but is held by the roots wrapped around her neck.

I lunge forward, thrusting down with the blade to sever the connection! The creature did not falter, only leaping away with the girl still attached and screaming. The loud cries swiftly ended as her eyes turned towards the back of her skull. "l-leave—us alone!" she demanded under the creature's mind control.

I charged after them as they exited through the front door! And into the fields, we trekked. Trapped in this void of leaf and vine, I lose sight of the two. Soon, realizing I am the one being hunted down... I can hear them—crawling around me. I try to predict their movement and jump out of harm's way. There was an error in my approach, and now I lay on the ground with the creature ready to strike.

The vines wrap around my neck as the sword in my hand is firmly grasped! "I can't have you chase us any longer, preacher!"

I would never allow myself to die, not here, not ever. With my left still free, I grabbed the vine, wrapping it around my fist, then began pulling with every bit of strength this damn body of mine has! He tried to hold on to Isabella with all his might! I had to end this bastard—eventually, I was able to rip him off and pull him in my direction! I don't know what entity inside would dare commit such an action, and yet, with this opportunity, I took it with a great bite! Chomping the upper half from the lower. His blood gushes between my teeth as the eyes flicker against my tongue. His screaming finally ceased once I tore the two sides...

The roots release their hold on me. I spat out his head and took a moment to catch my breath... The taste of copper stains my tongue—I require a stiff drink... I must take the girl back to safety. She is fortunate enough to be alive, simply unconscious from the shock. I lifted her around my arms and took her back home, where Cresalin guided me.

I take a moment to sit down, only to feel my body giving out and my eyes closing. My heart slows as this—head of mine drifts...

That dream was short-lived; I could only remember bits and pieces of those strange images—my actions. Opening my eyes, I saw the cobblestone ceiling and felt the familiar bed beneath me. The morning's light shines through the window, striking my weary eyes; such a burden could not outweigh the strains in my body. My legs, arms, feet, and head all soar from the previous night. I sat up on my bed to stretch my limbs carefully, and with a curious glance, I saw a platter of food on the table next to me. There was a note on the side with Cresalin's name etched at the bottom.

If you are reading this Phader. You do not have to worry about the family any longer. They now rest easy, thanks to you. The bread was specially made for you as a token of their gratitude... Be sure to rest easy and not stray too far from your bed. I shall return in time to help with your recovery.

I'm glad I was of some use to them... This bread has a delightful scent, making me eager to try it. Without hesitation, I took a bite, leaving the longing for respite absent... Before I rest, I should prepare my letter and send it to the capital; hopefully, they will not think of my words as lunacy. With evidence by my side, I will not have to worry about such things.

6

Within this body, I can only feel serenity... Partaking the flesh, I devour the final breath, exhaling into the moon's glow. My heart beats a beautiful melody—such a connection intertwines with the soul and body. Serenity, I say again... I open my eyes, and the red wine drops from her lips as her bright soul departs. There is not a single blink, a single shrug, nor a damn change of expression.

"Phader..." A voice calls for me. Is it my creator? Or the voice of many apparitions that choose to remain here in my world? Filling my head with a dreadful sense of discomfort. "Wake up, Phader." My mind stirs with an unsettling thought—I wake with the help of Cresalin, who stands by my side. She smiles as she looks down with her peering eyes... Her company brings me a slight joy in this sickly state.

She continued: "I was beginning to worry about you. Even in your rest, you still turn persistently."

"Yes, my dreams have been—an 'experience' to put it lightly." Truly, I could not explain that moment in the dream world, only an unease—sundry with a dotted dose of ecstasy.

"Well, we are going to have a lot of time together. Maybe you can try telling me what you saw."

I replied: "There is not much for me to say; I'd rather keep it personal... But tell me, why are you going to stay here with me? Doesn't the others need your assistance?"

She smiles sincerely again, "Do not fret, Phader. I wish to aid you in any way I can and—with those dreams of yours. Something could happen in your unconscious state."

"Such as sleepwalking?"

"Or worse... But let us not dwell on that now. If you need anything, don't hesitate to ask. I will be over by the window indulging in my hobbies."

She wanders towards the other side of the room, resting in one of the chairs as the sun's pale brushes the curtain onto her lap, then takes a needle and thread, proceeding to crochet. It was a humble sight to see in the moment, only to be ruined by that familiar sensation, the one I had in that dream... Wanting to speak more to her, I had to hold myself back from doing so—worried I might strain her sympathy—the chance of burden seemed likely.

She returns her curious glance, "Is there something you need?"

I replied: "No... nothing of importance." I turned my body towards the wall while closing my eyes. For what seemed like hours, my mind found that inner peace, taking me into the next world.

It was not a new place where I drifted, but rather a memory entwined within a bizarre world. Wandering for moments at a time as the world skips from the single blink. A woman suddenly stands before me; she is about my height, particularly in her stance; sweet was her expression, her heart, however... It was something else. Cold as frostbite, nipping at the gloveless hands that dare hold out into the bitter air. A fine wine, she was on a first impression. Always she wanted to speak—but I never had the words to say... 'Am I a bore?' I questioned myself, or is her beauty too much to bear? A question I cannot answer... These times of—desolation take a firm hold on my mind. For am I a coward with no answer? Or a simpleton with no explanation... I cannot answer this question. My mind drifted into a fantasy of a romance that never existed, a sick tragedy it seemed when this love of mine was never meant to be. Sleeper will never permit it... Storing my destiny with a purpose I never asked for... I suppose it's for the best. In time, I may be answered or remain in a state of misfortune... A pain dwells within me, a sense of isolation. That same pain begins to differ from itself and becomes pleasure, a—masochism some would consider.

Upon this dank hall where I stand in solitude, my vision blurs with awful inconsistency—next to me, I see a woman sleeping in my bed. She has no hair, eyes, lips, ears—no, it was only a feminine figure. Raising her stance, she reveals her naked anatomy, expressing the motions seductively... She carefully pulls my hands against her smooth face, which pulses with life underneath the skin. Shapes formed around her, sockets for her eyes, cheekbones for her mouth, and strains of hair forming at the scalp. For a moment, she became someone I had seen before; within seconds, she changed into a different woman, only to repeat this process. The changes do not hinder her movements, but she is vigilant in pulling me in. I try to remain distant, finding the doorknob that leads out from this place... To my dismay, I could not find such an object or anything that would allow me to escape. As for the woman, she presses her naked body against mine. Pressing her fingers against my groin—I relented by pushing her away. Such rebellion will not deter this ambition. Still, she wanted me to join her. When I closed my eyes for a brief second, my body produced waves upon waves of vigor... My needs and desires overwhelm the rational part of me. When I open my eyes, I see her pressed against the bed with my hands wrapped around her wrists. My groin penetrates inside, connecting us in this twisted sense of ecstasy. I—I wanted all of it... This pain needs to be exhaled from my body—and this woman is the cure to my freedom.

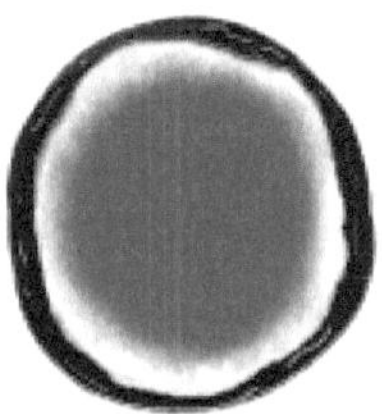

That lustful dream could never quench the ravenous urge in me, only perpetuating my hidden desire for companionship... Awakened in the dead of night, I twist under the covers. Turning to Cresalin, I see her sleeping on the chair with a lit candle by her side, giving life to her darkened gaze. Even in the darkest corner, with mysterious eyes and dark appearance, I still find her charm desirable. That thought of mine had to be removed, focusing on the act of sleeping—and yet, the thoughts persisted.

I question the very intentions I crave, wondering if there was any way to remove this burden. A Phader I am, a speaker of our lord, Sleeper. I try to remain focused on making this cathedral a home for everyone. Such intentions are held back due to this natural craving for love that—in a way, never existed or question to believe. I had attempted many times in the past to find this 'idea' of companionship, only to be left on the ground, with my inwards pulled and my face covered in scars... In metaphor, of course.

Within these many hours, I noticed that bluish light rising above my shadow, bringing forth the morning I had been waiting for. Risen from my bed, I had awakened Cresalin from the loud creaking it made.

She said calmly: "Morning, Phader. Did you sleep well?"

I replied: "I slept to some extent with unusual dreams."

"We should discuss more once I return with a warm drink."

Slowly, she reached the door, closing it behind her. As for me, I walk over to the window, looking at that silver ring in the sky as the sun rises from below... Sitting by the table, I became absorbed in my thoughts as I—tried to remember every detail of that dream. I often wonder about its obscure nature and why it fills me with this dread and—longing, trying to remain focused on the beautiful sight. Its persistence could not be detoured for a single moment besides Cresalin's sudden appearance.

She walked in with a tray in hand, placed it on the table, and poured a drink for the both of us. The steam waves into the air with such vigor as the smell enchants me to its bitter taste. She, too, glances at the sight before taking a sip.

"You look as if you're lost in thought," She noticed my plane expression.

"I usually am," I assured, "it's nothing out of the ordinary... How about you? Do you have any thoughts to share? Sleeping in your position must have been a burden for the body."

"It wasn't all bad... In truth, I don't sleep very much at all. Closing my eyes can only do so much for me."

"Do you have a condition?"

"Nothing you should be worried about, Phader."

"I'm afraid my condition persists that I worry for the people around me."

She gave a slight laugh, "It's alright. But if I require your help, I know you will be there for me."

We enjoyed a bit of silence before I moved on to the next topic, "How are the others fairing from my absence?"

She nods, "All are well now; they are worried for you. As for that stranger we met in the cave, the—Galik-Brusadore, he wants to speak to you."

"What for?"

"He did not say why... Alen had tried to get him to talk for a while now. You are the only one with whom he wants to speak. Only if you are able enough, of course."

"I had remained in bed long enough—walking will do me some good."

And in the dungeon, I lurked through the foul air and death's quivering anticipation. The rotting food and fecal matter drop into the cages as the prisoners stand against the wall, avoiding the impact. Towards the end, behind the reinforced door, the Galik-Brusadore sits at the corner, his cloudy gaze taunting me as if he were aware of my presence.

"Phader..." Galick spoke the first word, "Within this foul place, your odor is well defined. For there lies a secrecy..."

I take a moment to respond, "Do you know why you are in here?"

"Suspicions..."

"Your timing was very convenient. Sarian's journal contained foul entries and arts that defy our laws."

"He was... A devoted man. If he wanted something, he would do anything to take it."

"Such as taking little girls?"

Galik smirked, "We do not judge the needs of one another; it is our duty to allow total freedom for all. Your dedication to Sleeper keeps you from discovering yourself—discovering sensations you never knew existed."

"There is a reason we have to hold back," I replied sternly, "You can develop a sickness for these pleasantries, a sort of obsession that will destroy your life and the life of others."

"The words of Sleeper never cease to amuse me... You cannot change the thoughts of the many. Even if they did agree to your words, they would give in to those urges... That—sickness in you has come out sooner or later. That woman... Alen, they have such desires as well." He started laughing.

"I'm not going to amuse you anymore. Where are your followers?"

"It's hard to say, Phader. They are in places of familiarity, places of peace. Would you not want that for yourself? I cannot imagine why you would take away such luxuries."

"What pleasantries have you had for yourself? You don't serve your country through any means, nor do you feed the hungry mouths. Are you out there, only surviving on the fruit nature provides?"

"Of course... Nature blesses with riches for the empty gut and a surface to rest. As for—providing for the many faces, that is something only a weak-minded cretin such as yourself would say... Have you not been scoffed at by those around you? I have—many times before... Phader, this world has many forms of evil than you care to notice. How long do you have in this world before it beats you down and eats you alive? I wonder..."

"I see you are not willing to cooperate with me, Galik. I shall allow you to rot in your cell for eternity."

"Do what you must. At least I will be at peace far more than you will ever be."

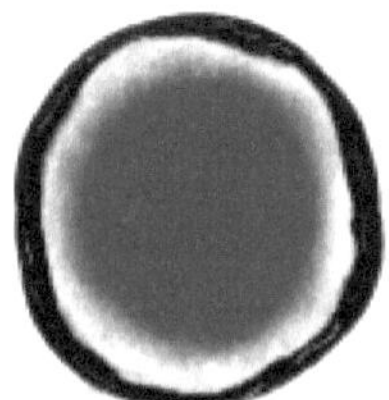

The day darkens with its warm light descending over the horizon. The shifting of light transfixes against my skin as I drink; I knock it back until the last drop enters my body... My mind is lost in the abyss as I stand in isolation, still exhausted from the previous night. This burden of mine runs deeper than anything I could have imagined. Is the life I have with these people little compared to that of love? Is it not enough for me to inspire many minds? Kneeling at the foot of my bed, I stretch my arms forward and whisper: "Sleeper... These thoughts you have given me, why can I not turn them away through desires alone? I wish to only serve this realm for the greater good and nothing more. Please, take these thoughts away from me. Let me concentrate..." I sank further into my bed, shivering as those thoughts persisted. The sickness... Galik told me that, is this the symptom he was talking about something else? I need to find a way to control it.

And when I slept through the restless night, the pain clawed my body with vicious intent. The temptation rose higher than it had ever been—these damn fantasies began taking control of the rational part of me! Controlling such tempting dreams can never simmer if I crave a woman's touch... Cresalin, to be exact. Such a foul thing to lust over my colleague, my dear friend—and yet, the urge lingers on like a parasite that feeds on me, then gives me strength to move forward. Love was created to be a cruel antidote...

When I awoke from that thought, that—uninterrupted state of agitation, sleep be damned from my intentions... A soft blue light crawled into my bed chambers, pointing me to gather my modest clothing and head out into the cobblestone labyrinth. Instead of joining the others in the company, I took the time to clean the areas that were left unkept. Broom in hand, I swept for hours, pushing away the gathered filth from the causal glance. My focus turned elsewhere when I reached the temple. Gothic architecture amazes me even now, though I have seen it many times before. But when I heard those familiar steps behind me, that pain haunted me once more.

"My-my..." Cresalin said suddenly, "You are more proactive this morning than most."

"I am..." I replied, fixing my eyes on the environment. "It would be better to keep this clean so our minds can have time to focus on more important matters."

"At this rate, Phader. You are going above the necessary. Would you rather reserve your strength for greater matters?"

I take a moment to consider her words, "You are right, Cresalin... These matters have gotten the best of me. My mind is a curious one to cure."

"I can't imagine your thoughts, especially when you spoke with Galik."

"I don't have much worry for him. He's imprisoned, after all... I am more worried about his followers, and will fate bring them to me at my worst?"

"Why do you fear them?" she asked, "They are nothing more than the common bandit. Although I must admit, I find it strange how they search for freedom when Sleeper permits us to have it."

"That cult, excuse me—the followers of Hettalies believe Sleeper only gives us a fragment of freedom. Which isn't the case. Our minds are completely free, and our will can have many opportunities. Our order is about filtering the morals of our actions. Galik and his believers believe no filter should be considered, and morality be damned in their case."

"Hettalies... I have heard something about her long ago, but the name was taboo."

"It still is," I confirmed, "The goddess of autonomy. The one who wished for total freedom... The Phader's before I will only speak harshly of her name, and many will scorn the flesh of those seek for her words."

"Why would she be hunted down for this idea of—true freedom?"

"The actions that were made from this idea turned the kingdom into a state of catastrophe. Why would you help your neighbor if their goods are worth taking for yourself? Why work the farms to feed the many hungry mouths when you can drink and live within your fantasies... Damn to all that is good-natured. The selfish will strive... The followers of Hettalies have brought our kingdom to chaos... It was from that part of time when the many realize that true freedom corrupts those capable of great evil."

"Who is capable of great evil?"

"Anyone..." I answered, "It does not matter if you are rich or poor, strong, or weak. If you can produce good in this world, you also have the power to create wickedness. Thus, a filter must be made to keep the balance of society. Even if it means Galik and his people must be imprisoned... For they might begin the cycle once more, and our society will be brought to a second collapse."

"Why would she want this freedom to begin with?" She asked.

"She is a servant created by Sleeper himself; like many of his creations, she was supposed to be the keeper of this realm, a watchful eye. She did not believe that a mortal should remain seated to an orthodox. 'Life offers many fruits,' she said in the written scriptures."

"You know your history well..." she said, surprised.

I shifted myself away, "I learned well in my youth..."

"You speak like an old man," she jested, "Are you not the same age as I?"

"We are... They say I am still youthful, yet my mind is a spoiled apple in the sun."

"You are different from the other Phaders. Not even they would consider the thoughts of those around them."

"It is better to learn from those around you... I hope to learn more."

Cresalin's lips rose as her face slowly turned red, "I can teach you many things myself—Karthuras."

Admittedly, it shocked me when she said my name.

"I—I am sorry, Phader. I—"

"It's alright..." I reassured with a smile pressed against my face, "It's the first time anyone has said my name in recent memory..."

55

7

A month had passed since I had arrived here, and already I had encountered strange anomalies and dealt with strange minds... The previous Phader had mentioned such things in his journals—that I glanced in speculation. Experiencing these contentions, I know there is some truth to these encounters. I wondered if the journals I sent to the Archphader would place me through a similar fate...With that in mind, I persist in the present. The morning passed as I and Cresalin met with the family again to investigate for any disturbances. Thankfully, no issues were found; their daughter Isabella now looks healthier than previously... We gathered around the table as we drank the delightfully hot bitter drink, discussing stories of embarrassment and laughing at the absurdity. What made this experience more appealing—was the delightful smell of freshly baked bread spiced with herbs and other sense burners. My stomach turns from such an aroma.

Within those blissful moments, I made a grave mistake that made our moods sourer than they ought to have been. That curiosity had itched my mouth to question the other family on the other side of the field... Felga, Dereks's wife. She pondered whether it should be answered.

She elaborated: "Sometime during harvest, we had noticed the two hiding in their shed as their son played with our daughter... I thought it was strange that the two would go off and reject their duties... So, I walked over and tried to offer them some help with their harvest," She shivered with a cold stare, "Beyond the door, I saw the two praying to the demon Hettalies."

My fingers twitched; already, I knew where this was going.

Felga continued: "Then, I saw the husband with a slit throat, blood rushing down his neck as his wife was holding the blade in her hand."

"How terrible..." Cresalin gasped.

"The ritual of true freedom..." I commented, rubbing my chin nervously, "Taking their own lives so Hettalies will lead them to true freedom. To—to start again in a new form."

"Why would they do such a thing!?" Felga asked furiously, "They were good people..."

I glanced at the black liquid within my wooden mug, "Sometimes. Those who want peace will find a disease they never knew existed. Perhaps their wishful thinking led them into a state of torment. They must have grown tired and worried about their future. Did they mention anything about regret?"

"None of the sort," Derek answered.

I asked a second question: "What of their son? I'm sure he must have said something curious."

"I don't recall..." Felga answered.

"Now, for my final question... Why is the son still in her company?"

"He doesn't want to leave her..." Isabella answered.

"We had tried to take him away," Derek said with a nervous tug of his tunic, "No matter how hard we tried. He finds a way to return home in his mother's arms."

"We did receive the word of the unfortunate circumstances," Cresalin added to the conversation, "But our interference could bring a terrible burden to the chapel. The crops are vital for our survival in the winter. If we tore them away, we could fall behind on our supply…"

"This is most unfortunate…" I replied.

They became followers of Hettalies, paying the price for a new beginning. The mother and her son remain on the field, tending to their crops and supplying the chapel as winter draws near. I can't imagine how hard the labor must be with fewer hands to help in their situation… An idea appears in my mind, and a willingness to help those in need removes the thought of a counter. As the day progresses, Cresalin returns to the chapel, tending to the needs of her people as I remain in the fields to meet with the mother and son.

Holding the scythe in her two hands, she cuts the wheat from the stem with a single stroke. The son uses a smaller one, holding the grain firmly with his left hand while the other cuts.

"Greetings…" I introduced myself.

"Is there something we can do for you, Phader?" She asks, placing the tool by her side, "We will have everything ready by the end of the month."

I smile sincerely, "I am not here to rush your labor; I am here to give you an extra hand." "What for? Do you not have other problems to deal with…?"

"There are many, but—I can use some of my spare time to help with your situation."

"I don't have time to teach you the tricks…"

I wave my hand, gesturing reassured, "There is no need for me to learn. I've experienced many forms of labor; this will be no different."

I walk towards the shed with a dusty scythe taken from the rack. The mother's face turns stern momentarily, then eases her thoughts when she watches me maneuver through the harvest... Eventually, the mother and son catch up with their side until they finish one of the rows.

"I must admit..." The mother said, breathless, "You know your way around tools. How does a farmer become a Phader?"

"I was no farmer..." I replied, "I had tended to the fields a few times but never stayed long enough to own the property."

"You were a 'labor mixer?' finding job after job until something sticks with you."

I gave a slight laugh, for there was truth. "No, the Archphader demanded of me to gather experience working with the people I swore to guide."

She looks at me curiously, "Were you here for money? If so, I have none to give."

"That also wasn't my intention, I can assure you, and—if you allow it, I can return tomorrow and help with the next row."

"Alright then..." She said regretfully.

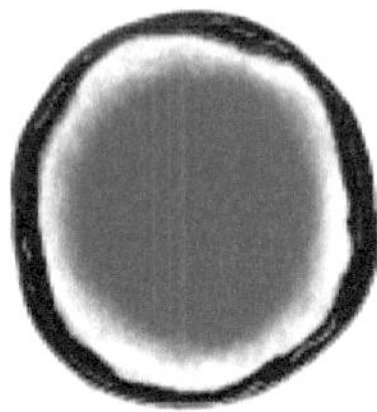

Day after day, I tended to those crops, from early morning to the night's stillness. Determined I am to finish the endless labor. My further absence from the cathedral was not vain, however—Cresalin, my colleague, attends to her people's needs with a mother's embrace... During my time here, I also tried to communicate with the widow, only speaking plainly about her provenance—she remained silent as expected. The actions are a different point of discussion, like a bizarre riddle.

Her face becomes red, with dry tears staining her cheeks, during times of rest. Unblinking, she was staring at her son while clenching onto him. Relieving the burden of mental anguish... While I continued working, she would sneak into the shed and softly close the door behind her. Acting on my curious nature was strange, but I relented by sneaking over to the shed, gazing through the cracks.

Isolated from the world, the widow nurtures a tiny sprout with a strange shade of color. They're usually the same as the grass; conversely, this sprout is dark and crimson, like a drop of blood.

I would check the sprouts' progress every night, noticing the obscure changes. A part of me knows the obscure flora contains a deep malice that could danger the widow, her son, and myself... Burdened by the question of discovery—I... I wanted to see it bloom for myself, but I am no fool when it comes to consequences, knowing it would be beneficial to prepare myself for danger. I am neither an expert in combat nor a strategist.

I had taken a dagger from my chest that was—rusted from the lack of care. Strange, I do not recall using it recently. In truth, I had never used it in defense. To my astonishment, the second collapse never came to the capital—in which I never had a reason to use it... A part of me Knew I should bring one of the knights with me in case these matters become more complicated. Their extent, on the other hand, will help bring Hettalies followers forth a rebellion to their cause, making these matters overwhelming—Thus plaguing me with a grim perspective of our future.

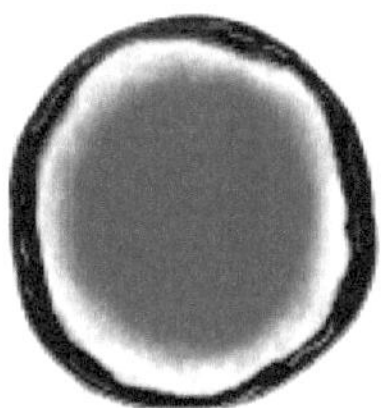

The pale sun hovers over my head, burdening my mind with a staggering perspective. The longing for time takes its toll on the working soul wanting to be freed of the repetition and onto more—personal matters... 'Time' has always been my greatest teacher. Wasting your precious moments in youth will only burden the elder self into perpetual dread—left in the grave, rotting in regret...

Earlier, I made a short visit to the Gravis family for a loaf of herbal bread. The smell tempted my famished stomach as I wrapped it in a fine cloth.

I walked over to meet with the widow and her son. Knocking on their door, I wait patiently and smile genuinely at their presence. The mother opened the door as I asked: "May I come in?" To my surprise, she nodded in response, allowing me to enter.

The three of us gathered at the table with a bowl of broth. The smell was earthy, with traces of meat. Stirring my spoon, I noticed the sliced potato slices and bits of chicken. I take a few untainted sips, finding the dish pleasurable for the tongue. Eventually, we all combined the bread, finding the mixture suitable. Their sharp reactions were more noticeable than mine—surely, they enjoyed it more than I did.

The mother was silent for a while, but her eyes shifted back to the table and towards me. Her lips wanted to utter... With a deep breath, she eventually spoke: "Thank you for everything you've done for us in the past three weeks..."

I reframed himself from eating another piece from the loaf, as I replied: "I'm glad I could be of service."

"I could never understand why you do this for everyone in the chapel... Are you a masochist?"

I slightly chuckled at the comment, "This is my purpose..." I wipe the crumbs from my lips, "Everyone needs a helping hand, especially under their conditions. Should I not offer a bit of service?"

"Showing kindness to others is a sign of weakness..." she replied, "A man like you should know of such things. Would it not be better to be free from the bindings that hold you?"

"The only one who binds I—is myself. If I were to allow myself to be free. I could perform evil acts upon the both of you." Her brow rises as her hands steer towards her knife. "I can see your reaction..." I continued, "If you were to remove the filter of your decisions, a feeling of bliss will come present. The long-term will come with a great ordeal of pain... It will appear when you least expect it to."

She eased her hand before she replied, "What about everyone else who does share the same idea of morality? Nobody cares about you or me—or my husband," She covers her lips to prevent further speaking.

"Everyone has their own stories," I said, "And yes... People have done me wrong more times than I can count. In time, I was able to learn to forgive their ignorance."

"Their—ignorance?" she questioned.

"Sometimes, people do not pay close attention to their actions. Like feral dogs, they must fight for survival... Sometimes—they strike the weak without knowing it. That fear of theirs turns to absolute ignorance, which is why I can forgive them."

"Are you not angry from the pain they inflicted of the pain they caused you!?"

"I was... but how can one rise if they don't know how to fall?" I lean over the table, "You have two choices to make when inflicted with such scars. You can use the pain as a form of strength—or allow it to evolve into a parasite feeding on your body... What will you choose?"

"They should all be damned, Phader!" The mother said ferociously. "They can all burn! No one will hurt us anymore..." She takes a moment to calm herself, "You should leave this place and never return..."

I did not speak further, worried I might dampen my social status towards a terrible state. I felt the bitter silence leaving the house behind me—but I did not return to the cathedral. Instead, I ventured to the forest's edge and waited. Waiting for her to visit the curious flora in her shed, with her son held by her side, they walk inside that dark shed...

For a moment, I waited until the whaling veiled through that open door. The tone secretes agony... With the dagger firmly in my grasp, I lowered myself and crept towards the shed. Peering around, I see the two standing before the sprout—now taller than my previous inspection.

The whaling cries begin once more beneath the surface. The mother takes the boy's hand and then slits his palm, then her own. Together, they drip the blood onto the foul stem, allowing the plant to drink.

"Rise again, my love…" she said, "Let us rejoice—let us become whole again."

A large head of flesh and vine reveals itself—the flesh covering the skeletal structure, roots extending in every direction. Something appears within the flesh petals; it opens like a flower in bloom; the core is substituted with a torn human head.

"Darling!" The mother cried out. A part of her wanted to walk closer to the abomination, but a fragment wanted to keep distance, thus remaining a few feet away from her reanimated husband.

"Tel—la…" The head turns to the son, "Jar—o…"

The two were speechless… I, too, am staggered by the sight… Resurrecting the dead from their eternal slumber from the land of dreams is profound. None would consider the idea!

"My—loves…" The creature mutters in agony, "Why would—you torture me so? Why—Tella, did you not join—my death?"

She grovels on her knees, "I'm sorry, darling. I would have joined you… But I was surprised by our neighbors my—my mind was elsewhere!"

"I—forgive you…" The roots from his flesh begin pouring onto the surface like snakes. "When I tear your flesh, I shall sow the many seeds—into your carcass!" The vines grab hold of her limbs!

She struggles to escape their grasp; her efforts are in vain. Their son reaches for the roots, attempting to break his mother free!

I rush in with the dagger held high in my grasp and the blade directed at the head of this creature, plunging the edge inside the skull!

The creature cries with a disformed resonance: "The—Blood!" The monster yelled, "Give me blood!"

The vines swarm around the mother's limbs, then sprouted thorns from the surface and dug deep into her body—soaking the essence from her flesh.

I pulled the dagger out and then drove back again! My efforts had no effect against him—as for his wife, her body was weakening as the skin became pale, and the eyes sank deeper into her skull. With haste, I take the boy away from the shed before he shares a similar fate, a fate the boy had already contracted. The vine had wrapped around him as his blood began to drain from his body. I fell on my back and crawled out from the shed, watching as the creature drained his son...

My options are limited to the death of this creature, but to kill such a thing is the point of discussion. An idea did emerge in my mind, leading me to the house, taking the oil-filled lantern, and returning once more to the shed.

The creature removes himself from the soil and then begins walking towards me. With the lantern in my grasp, I toss the object inside, closing the door soon after. I pressed my back against the door as I felt the monster's weight pushing from the other side.

The fire spreads from within. The smoke progresses through the door's cracks and the smell of char sterns my nostrils. The howling blends with the orchestra of flames that consume everything within!

When his efforts subsided—I walked away from the door while the flames exhausted the structure... During this night, I tremble on my knees, gazing at the fire, wishing I could do more for the family and save everyone from that terrible fate. But no matter which direction I gazed; their fates would have led them to their deaths. Still—a terrible guilt corrupts my soul. All I can do now is pray: "S-sleeper who watches us from the great ring... Guide their souls into your land of dreams so they may find peace..." The smoke rises into the atmosphere, leaving a black trail slithering into the silver jaw, thus ascending into the void.

8

"These walls contain riddles only a few can hear... Listen carefully to the words and heed their meanings, for they will not listen to you. They will not dare ask why or partake in company. They will only give and expect you to take... Once the words are spoken, you must ask the questions and conserve your thoughts... It would be best if you questioned my words. Are they worthy of one's thoughts, or are they the ramblings of a fool writing in his book? I will let all of you decide that for yourselves..."

I spoke to the residents about the false preachers of our world. Phaders or Galiks who speak with good intentions—using their influence to pursue devious rewards. Even I do not know much of myself or what evil I can perform when unconscious to those in the crowd sitting with their thoughts tangled.

Together, they left the room, leaving only the subtle whispers of words I could barely understand. For my last offering of today, I strolled to the confession booths. The designs of these structures were always a favorite of mine to admire: Around the edges of the roof, lines of string hung loosely with silver rings—and the walls contained a black fabric with stars flickering inside the abyss with their vibrant glow.

Entering inside, I adjusted the velvet sheet and rested myself against the wall, waiting for strangers to arrive and speak from their occupied minds... Of which, my monologue kept my attention away from the stranger. "Phader, it has been a while since we last spoke..." The feminine voice was the one from before. "Have you thought of me ever since our last encounter?"

I replied: "I do not know who you are—nor should I."

"Why hide yourself from me, Phader? Are you not here to help those in need and bring peace to this place? I—I'm losing control of my body..." She sticks her fingers through the gate. "Please—please take this pain away, Phader. Allow your body to meld with mine."

"Your devotion to me is unnatural... That mind of yours is holding a foul image—perhaps a foul time in your history... Please do not tempt me with such thoughts."

Her fingers retract, "You shouldn't hold back so much; how much pain can you endure, Phader? The prospect tempts you, but your faith is holding you back from the true pleasure of the soul."

I said sternly: "My faith has helped me and the many from disorder. Would you give me this pain once more? Does it give you pleasure?"

"The pain is becoming worse... Will you open the door? I can ease your sorrow."

My hands quiver as they reach for the handle, "No..." I whisper to myself.

These temptations of lust are destroying me from the inside greater than before—I had to remember the words of our order, keeping myself firmly under control. 'Thou must take the words of commitment and remove false promises. The pain to endure is a sanctuary to those in need.' It is better to suffer now than later.

"Will you open the door?" she prompted me.

"N-no..." I replied with an exhale.

"Why continue to hold yourself back, Phader? Do you not deserve a night's rest in the company of a woman, removing the burdens if only for a moment? Will you not take the bosom of someone who cares for you?"

My damn nature demands to give in—still, I must contain myself, "If you truly cared for me. You would not torture me after my answer... No, you are starving for something. You seek only for my audience—and once I am used up, you will soon move on to the other and repeat the process..." There was no whisper, a single breath, or another word said. She had suddenly left.

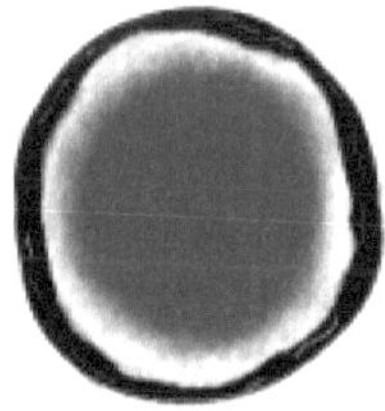

I needed relief from this eternal pain—it was stagnant, persistent in ways of inconvenience! The desire for one's companionship presses against my soul like a parasite gnawing my rational desire, then leaving dung in its wake... Strolling through these desolate halls leaves too much for my imagination to transpire. For a moment, I thought my crazed mind was creating an illusion... Before me, on the cobblestone wall—a layer of liquid swirls. With a simple touch from my finger, the current's once calm swirl ripples a barrage of rings swaying towards the edge. It did not stain my finger in the slightest...? Just a comfortable sensation against my skin.

This anomaly became fascinating from every touch I had given to its curves. My mind loosens the chains holding that dreadful part of me... Suddenly—I could feel a blend of madness swarming my thoughts. It occurred to me that this anomaly anticipates my arrival, and I'm only delaying myself from its entrance. Allowing myself to enter the void in this state produces an overwhelming state in my imagination. Indeed, the chance of danger is definite—Alas, my anguish needs respite.

And the throbbing needs to churn out from this tight apparel! My darling, are you waiting for me on the other side? Without a second thought to waste my precious time, I enter through the void to see the other side—to see what pleasures await me—and at Awe, I came upon seeing such a magnificent sight! Against the wall, the feminine physic mangles in the plethora of limbs that allure the malnourished. The Velvet carpets do wonders to grasp my wondering gaze. Her hand arises from the dark crevices—protruding further than usual, while the skin detracts to shape into long fingers. Pressing her hand against my body, I feel shocked in relief from the pain. My oh my—she teases my beastly shadow of desire, begging me to ravage her soft skin! Why would I allow myself to hold back? Wasn't it Sleeper who had given us these delightful creatures?

I open my eyes to the red—flowery carpet. The morning has dawned in my absent state... Battered and exhausted from the previous night, I stand up in a daze, wondering about those visions, that—creature from the wall... From a simple gesture, I felt a slight shock underneath the skin, aching from its consistent use. I can no longer concentrate thoroughly; I must proceed back to my quarters and rest adequately.

9

The winter has arrived—bringing upon these lands its chilling pale sheet while the mist blinds the sight miles wide. To keep warm, I quench my insides with the alcohol I find scattered down in the cellar. My long strolls through the corridors can only do so much as these thin windows contain no barrier to the cold air. With a simple glance outside, I see something moving... A wagon pulled by two black stallions with fabrics covering their backs. Has a Phader arrived at the chapel at this time of year? I had not received a letter about such a visit. I headed for the main door, where Cresalin and her helpers were already greeting our guests.

She stood presently with a welcoming gesture, then invited the strangers into the main hall... As I approached the group, the modest welcoming had already turned sour. The Phader known as 'Horton' splurges unthankful words towards my colleague: "My dear, I am considered a prophet to many people of this fine country. If I am not presented with wine and—"

The man beside him grabbed the Phader's shoulder, urging him to calm down: "Please, Phader Horton. This lady welcomed us in without question. You could say 'Thank you' at the very least."

I walk forward with my greeting: "Welcome, Dr. Krill and Phader Horton," I said eagerly, "It is a surprise to see the two of you here—especially in the winter."

Dr. Krill walked forward with a long smile against his sunken face, shaking my hand as he spoke: "Phader Karthuras, it has been a long time since I had seen that damn beard of yours!" he chuckled.

I replied: "I had always kept it firmly trimmed over these past months."

"Enough of these—pleasantries," Horton intruded: "I am tired from the cold and bumpy roads! My pecker is shriveled and may fall off any moment."

To keep my—limited hospitality, I lead the two with Cresalin by my side. She walks forward with a stern expression. Horton had already left a negative impression on both of us; however, I had already expected it to be the case due to his insecurities. He was first to be considered Phader for this Cathedral, only for me to be chosen instead... Only the three of us gathered by the fire at one of the tables as the servants prepared a small meal. Tempted, Cresalin was to sit by my side, but the foul first impression from the Phader made her walk elsewhere for the time being.

Before she left, she whispered in my ear: "I shall prepare a place for them to rest in. But if the Phader speaks anymore, I shall leave him outside in the cold..." Her spitefulness worried me.

I turned my attention back towards our guest: "Normally, the capital would send a letter of one's arrival. Especially the presence of a fellow Phader..."

Dr. Krill responded: "I'm afraid these matters are private. We cannot have a commoner read the letters and turn those words into gossip for the public. You and I both know the dangers that could cause."

"You... Have you read my letters to the Archphader?"

Horton grins, turning the fat folds of his face while speaking: "Oh yes, Phader. We have read these—interesting riddles of your anomalies and wench malformities... Such tales could place you in a noose if read by the wrong set of eyes."

Dr Krill looks at me with discomfort, "I'm sorry about this intrusion. I did not wish for it, having no choice under this circumstance."

Before I could curse Horton for this—act of betrayal, our drinks had arrived, and so had our meals. Alas, the anger boils inside me, detracting the sense from simple pleasures. Krill could not touch his food either as Horton dug in with restless fervor... I had to drink to calm these nerves from further expansion. Thankfully, it did not take long for us to join my study.

I was the first to break the bitter silence: "Phader Horton, what provokes a coward's way of negotiation? What is it you're after?"

Horton chuckles again under his breath, "Oh Karthuras, how long I have waited for this moment to see that calm face stern with a fiery lust for blood. I will never forget this moment!"

Krill commented, "I would not worry about such affairs, Karthuras. We are here for other reasons besides politics."

I ask: "What other reason could you have?"

Horton replied: "To answer the greatest question we all ask ourselves when no one is looking," he leans forward, "To see Sleeper himself... To see if such a being truly exists. When I read those letters, the contents regarding the conjuring arts prompted the idea. You may rejoice to know my death draws closer by the day—and before I die—I must witness the answer for myself. I will be remembered as the man who observed the other side and returned to the mortal realm."

"Are you dull from your old age, Horton? Do you wish for our order to brand us as heretics?"

Horton replied: "Do not whine, youngling... I shall take the fall if the question were to arise. There is no point in me destroying your reputation if there is nothing to keep in the long term. In fact, you should thank me—by licking the boots that grace your floor... But that's enough for me; I have bottles to empty before this night ends. I expect our plans will be explored by tomorrow." He left the room.

I had to rest deeper in my chair, allowing the bitter sensation to course through me. Still, I needed more answers from my—friend; I hesitated to say: "What is your arrangement with that bastard? Are you not an atheist?"

Krill took a swig from his flask before he spoke: "That—I still am, for now, to be given such an opportunity is a rare treat to devour. It's hard to look away... But I was not given this opportunity respectfully, no—he threatened my livelihood and prepared his servants to brand me a heretic, following the ways of Hettalies... Believe me, I did not want us to reunite under these conditions."

"I can tell you're distressed from this affair, and yet—there is something I should mention... I have indeed researched the minimal exploits of this—strange power, but I have no intentions of using it. Sarian had only the basic framework for me to learn from and only one conjure to put into practice."

"From the contents of your letters, it seemed to work in his favor."

"He could transfer his soul inside a commodity, true as it was at the time. However, to bring someone back from the dead is—speculative, to say the least."

"Does the framework you mentioned not contain the fundamental understanding for you to practice?"

"I also mentioned my limited involvement with this knowledge... I do not wish to practice such—wicked..." I had to stop myself before ranting about its implications and the time I spent with these anomalies.

"You don't have much choice in this matter as I," Krill mentioned, "Horton is more than willing to destroy our social standings and rid us into the countryside—or by the noose around our necks."

I hesitated: "If our choices are limited as you say, then I shall—dive deeper into this—abyss of lunacy."

"We shall discuss more of this tomorrow, Karthuras. Remember, if you need my help, do not hesitate to ask."

"I shall keep that in mind."

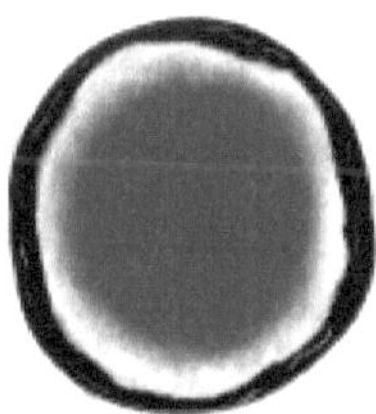

This task lingered in my skull like a damn—parasite. For a month, I handled my research with absolute precision (within my spare minutes, of course.) Such lengths I had dived into the unnatural bending of the material world... The only times of peace I've had were through Cresalin's persistence to care for my agitated state. Simple as it may seem, to feel an ounce of peace from the bitter drink she often brings. At times, I wondered if her presence was nothing more than an illusion in my mind, conjured to balance my sanity—before I fell into that swarming state of paranoia...

This is what I have learned thus far: these arts are performed under the strict rules of sacrificing the body or the life that dwells within it (a hard choice to make in the short term); either the body is repurposed, or the soul is removed from this plane of existence... I had mentioned this rule to both Horton and Krill—who remain ambitious... Dr Krill assures me that this medical procedure will control the contents of his life, allowing my efforts to have less strain. I'm afraid to say such comfort cannot be afforded; instead, I had to devise a plan that would guarantee some level of success. From the very words of Sarian himself: 'Taketh the soul from the body and deliver upon the rotting corpse. What keeps the body whole is the essence of life previously departed.'

I had one more point to take from this consultation. From the very man who is held, rotting in the dungeon. The Galik-Brusadore... Entering his cell, I find him against the wall, covering the contents of his festered skin. It does not take an intellectual to see the man is dying from the current state I had placed him in.

"W-what is it you want!?" Galik demanded an answer.

"I wish to know more of these conjuring arts—including its consequences."

Galik laughs violently with a graveling rumble in his throat, "Have you grown curious about the ideas of true freedom!?"

I replied: "I only wish to experiment with this concept."

"I won't tell you anything! Anything at all... How dare you ask of me after leaving me here for months! All I've had to eat—is dung falling from above my head... May you rot in the realm of nightmares for the rest of eternity!" Lunacy had corrupted his mind. It was pointless to ask such a simple question, and I would have granted him a mercy killing if he were to answer simply. A waste of effort, this was...

There was one last thing I needed to do: Equipping blades and amour. My skills in these tools are nonexistent. Even when I tried to fight that monster on that unfortunate day with the widow and her son, almost slicing my hand from my lack of grip...

I had begun wishing for the chance to burn Sarian's book of the Conjuring arts—while strolling down the corridors with Phader Horton and Dr. Krill. With the knowledge I had obtained, a certain darkness looms behind me—or perhaps it's the paranoia overwhelming my thoughts. To speak truthfully, practicing this art among my colleagues terrifies me. Every action we take comes with consequences—thus, will I be tempted to experiment further?

We had made it to the lower depths of the cathedral. Through the darkness, we enter the next room, with flagstone walls and planks left to rot under the humid atmosphere. The twitching of the slowly dying rat—did not spark any sense of confidence... Dr. Krill lays out a bed roll for Horton to lie upon, then digs into his bag to find the needed tools. Strangely, he takes out a curious leather mask: Its design contains a single silver ring around the face, held within the leather folds, while the leather within the ring is cross-stitched, allowing the wearer to have sight of the operation. I ask: "Is it wise to wear it during the procedure?"

Krill replied: "I can see just fine... I can't have the sweat of my brow dripping into Horton's innards."

Horton added: "And it would be wise to see Sleeper's ring in my final moments. Even if it's just a mask..." he coughed.

As they continued the preparations, I took a moment to secure this room. There were no other exits besides the door we entered through. With a strand of rope, I could tie the door handles together... Then I reminded myself of my current gear—taping the sheathed dagger around my belt and feeling the cold steel of my chest plate and—the potato hidden underneath.

"Do not worry, Karthuras," Krill reassures, "Will you remove that rope and put aside your dagger? You're making me nervous."

I replied: "The consequences of my actions might take a toll greater than us. Perhaps it could take over the cathedral..."

"I doubt Sleeper will interfere with our work. Does he not wish us to prosper and find the answers we seek?"

"That is a part of the many lectures... I doubt we will encounter the very being that created us—rather... Well, I'm not sure of what we'll find."

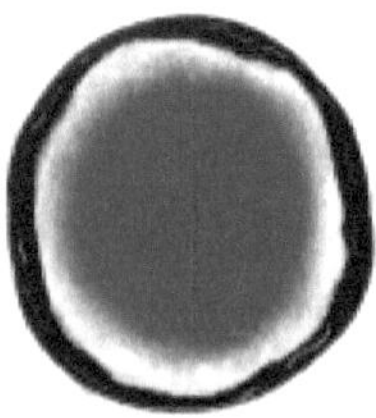

In my quarter span of life, I had never countered such sights committed under the pretense of medical dismemberment. A sight which regards the skin and takes the innards of oneself for operation. Horton consented to our colleague Krill committing such actions, but I don't think the old man truly comprehended this act. Fortunately, the doctor had a special potion to render the individual unconscious promptly. I watched the ghastly sight of the doctor splitting the flesh, stretching folds to reveal ribs until the heart was—exposed for all to see... As I tried to hold back my spew, the doctor placed a needle inside the old man's heart, injecting a serum. I asked about its contents, and in response, I was answered with 'Salt and sugar,' the two components needed to stop a beating heart—or at least simmer the rhythm into a dying state.

Blood spilled in liters with every moment spent on this operation; with the mask on, I could sense the Doctor feared his own capabilities. Even so, the perspective needed to satisfy the question of Sleeper's existence lingers on as our commitment... As he injects the serum into the beating heart—its rhythm decreases in the passing moment. The pale curtain is drawn over his lifeless body as the excrement passes into his undergarments. Dreadful the smell is...

Those small moments of our time are counted—making a minute. Within that minute, Krill uses both hands to press Horton's dying heart in a rhythm until it beats lively again. His efforts unfortunately had no sign of progress, thus acquiring me to perform the ritual. Hesitation pulsated through my thoughts as I considered this action, merely digging my grave for the terms of 'promise.'

Before I allowed the Phader to die, I had placed the spud near his body to allow the blood to flow onto its skin. Krill did not question this action and rather helped me lift the fat man's body. Once he leaned him over, I then chanted the words: "Taketh the soul from the body and deliver upon the rotting corpse. What keeps the body whole is the essence of life previously departed."

His blood slithers like worms exhaling from the soil, devouring the nearest morsel. Festering away at the spud—twisting and turning the body until a human-like face appeared.

Krill removes his mask, revealing his unnerved gaze, perplexed by this... for lack of a better term 'morbid-comedy.' He muttered: "Hor-horton...?"

Horton opened his eyes, hazy in his current state, "Krill... I—I had seen him... I had seen the endless dark..."

I lingered towards their side with my dagger ready to strike.

Krill pressed further: "Damnit, what did you see!? Tell me everything!"

Horton's eyes rolled side to side as his teeth began chattering, "My soul was carried away from my body, past the stone walls and into the night sky. I could see the stars as an ocean of darkness surrounded me. Then I saw him, floating with his hands stretched out, the dark hood showing me true oblivion. The nothingness... I had no control of my path; the void was absolute, the destination. Before entering that abyss, I suddenly returned to this world to where I am now... Please, I beg of you—don't let me return!"

Krill steps back, "No—I don't believe it..."

I asked: "There is only darkness behind the shadow?"

"Nothing more..." Horton answered, petrified.

My fears grew profoundly as the moments passed, not even in silence where we were left to ponder this reality. I could sense a presence—it draws closer yet...

"It's coming for me! It's coming for me!" Horton shrilled.

Then, I could see something moving within the darkness at the ceiling. A silver ring, spinning as it gives a hollow cry... I wanted to run, and all be damned in my absence! Within that wide ring, I could see something else moving from within. Before long, it also emerged like a fish hook sinking into the bottom of the lake. Its structure wasn't human though—abstractly designed to be one, beyond the realm in which can grow and produce... It protrudes over to Horton, who remains in his perplexed state.

"Join with us—Horton..." The creature's voice echoes through the room with a deep rumbling tune. Its arms rip apart from the folds as the hands grab him!

"No, please!" Horton cried, "I don't want to go back! I don't want to see him! I don't want to see him! I don't want to see him!"

Those deafening cries did not hinder the creature's heart from changing action. It was re;lucted... When they transverse into the darkness again, the ring removes itself from this reality, leaving Krill and I astonished by this terrible event.

"There... There is nothing more for me to do," Krill cried, "Even in truth—I still don't know the answer..."

I replied: "We cannot allow this idea to spread among these walls. If they don't believe in the land of dreams, the people will forever remain in a nihilistic state of existence."

He turns to me, amazed by my comment, "Why would you keep this hidden!? Do you not understand what we could do with this answer? We can finally escape—truly be free from all corruption and disorder—finally, we can strive to become immortals."

"We still don't know what lies beyond the void. There is still a possibility that the land of dreams still exists."

"No!" Krill yelled, "I am tired of this religion...! Karthuras, you are a free thinker such as I—why will you allow these ideas to continue to sway your mind!"

"Because life is uncertain... Please, my friend—rise from your despair."

"I can't do that, Karthuras... The people deserve to know the truth of the afterlife."

As he made his way for the door—my anguish twisted my heart within a violent grasp, pulsating the very organ within a tight grasp. No words could utter beyond my lips... Why could he not listen to reason? Does he not understand the nature of our kind? Our kingdom will fall into ruin once more if he spreads the truth. Damnit to all! He left me with no other alternative... As he tries to unbind the rope holding the door in place—I take the dagger with a firm grasp, plunging the blade into the skull of my dear friend! He fell over on his side as the blood poured from his untethered flesh.

Tears ran down my eyes as I tried to keep myself planted on the ground, but this pain—this pain was too great for one to bear. I never wanted this to happen—no, I warned them of these consequences, and they chose not to listen. Why do they all choose the path of destruction? Perhaps I am the mad one here—I held myself back from the truth for too long, and now, I stand in desolation.

10

I became lost inside my head, speaking the tunes of philosophy—pondering if my actions were justified or plain foolish. I suppose the majority will figure out my murderers' actions with ill intent, and I believe their fears are at play... Restless I am at this very moment, I want nothing more but to rest till morning arrives. The truth to my stubborn mind is the past, my childhood, mainly when the followers of Hettalies spread the idea of 'true freedom' across the kingdom. I had to witness the barbaric practices both Men and Women possess. The woman will use their charm and figure to possess countless gold, sleeping with numerous men around them; depravity for long periods turned them into monsters themselves from their shameless actions. When the child was born into this world, they were murdered and left on the streets, allowing the beasts to tear their flesh away from the very bone... As for the men, competition comes into play as their unsatisfied desires are never quenched. Betrayal, adultery, rape, and the murder of innocent people became common. No longer could we help our neighbor, no—everyone takes everything for themselves, tossing others to the wayside... Morality was damned. For a while, my world was forever scattered with this plague until the Phaders arrived to make everything right again, but even in their presence, I could sense their darkness. Horton previously reassured the sentiment. In our order, few within our circle are warmed by the idea of dominance and living a pompous life. I suppose our stagnant culture is the root that grows this weed of disorder...

I open my eyes to the door opening from the other side of the room, where Alen (The knight who had led me to the cathedral) welcomes himself without permission. His boots emitted a loud thud with every step until he leaned over my desk...

After a few moments, he finally spoke: "It's been a long while since you checked on your people—preacher..." he said with a severe tone and breath reeking of hard liquor, "Your persistence to leave has been leaving me to wonder as of late... What is it that you do when no one is watching?"

I replied: "You speak as if I had committed a grave act."

"Don't play dumb with me, Preacher. Do you know how many people have disappeared in your absence?"

"I am not aware of any."

"Doesn't surprise me..." he scoffed, "Though Phader Horton and Dr. Krill come to mind... Did they say anything to you before they left during the storm?"

"Only a simple farewell."

"But why would they travel through that bastard of a storm? Any sensible man would have told them to stay until it finally clears... Now tell me—what about the burning shed? Why did we find you on the ground, groveling at the very sight? We knew you were helping the widow deal with her crops, but why were you there alone—in that state?"

"What are you trying to say, Alen?"

He replied: "I think you are a cold—heartless killer... I'm convinced you murdered your colleagues—Making me question further the disappearances. Since we stayed here the first night, I had to suspect you after that incident with Evelyne. Perhaps that cock of yours had been drowning in Cresalin's mere for too long—it would not surprise me if she were part of your damn schemes."

I replied: "I have nothing to do with the many disappearances, nor does Cresalin. I wander off, helping people who need my service and nothing more. I neglected my surroundings, but it wasn't because of ill intent."

"I will have the answer soon enough. My mercs are combing this cathedral as we speak—and in time, we will know the truth... I suggest preparing your manuscript before we hang that neck of yours." He did not say another word, instead leaving behind the unpleasant aura.

Not knowing the truth about these unfortunate events (besides my previous encounters). I am now left questioning that point of interest and—my future... Resolving this conflict is my top priority; unfortunately, I have not been given the proper tools. I may have to invest my spare time learning more about the conjuring arts and memorizing every corner of the cathedral. These corrupted ideas of mine are my only line of defense against Alen and his mercs. Innocent or not, I must find the truth before they do. What are the chances they give up on their search and deem me as the suspect with no evidence or planted for someone's political standing?

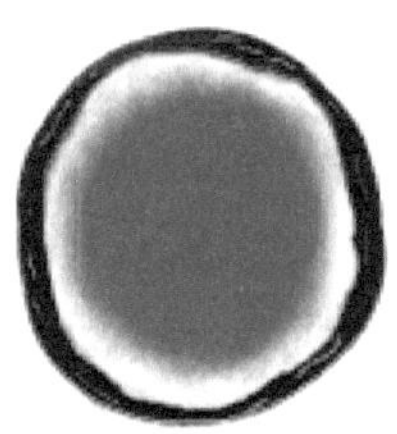

Under these conditions I had placed myself in, Alen's perception may have worsened from my choice of absolute privacy. I walked further than any into the depths until I could find a place that could guarantee my isolation from any curious wander. Only Sleeper knows how long I have spent in this rotten dungeon as I investigate my surroundings. Once I found a place deemed suitable for my research, I began reading the principles of conjuring...

I recited the words and chose the materials to start my experiment. Firstly, I had taken a lively mushroom, transferring its vitals into the rat's dead carcass with the phrase:

"Taketh the shell once belongs to the living—resurrect the conditions with the new," despite my thoughts of defeat, this worked to my favor... The shroom's vital essence transfers into the rat, turning the body and flesh towards the abstract. Though its lifeless eyes stare into the void, its body breathes with life as the shrooms within pulsate. Both living and dead, I had made this creature. I said to it: "Are you well, little rodent?" I did not get any response to my question. "Move forward, little rodent," I demanded. Still, no response is given. Perhaps I need to make another sacrifice and utter a new phrase. The previous shroom faded from the process, thus forcing me to make another sacrifice.

"Taketh the soul from the body—become one with the other, guiding the whims to my own," then I say again: "Move forward, little rodent," without a single flinch, it moves forward with haste until it stood on its little feet staring up towards my gaze. Now I wonder, 'How far will it give in to my demands?' To answer this question with a simple test, I tell it to eat the rotting shrooms. It devoured them without a shiver of response. I then told the creature to bang its head against the stone wall, and without question, it did so until the wall was stained with blood and spots of fur. The creature now lies dead from my demands, but I have concluded a simple idea: making it work on humans will be the real test. A test—I hope won't come to pass. I wanted to move forward with the next, but the lack of life around me hindered such progress, hence concluding my studies.

Carefully, I transverse back towards the central part of the cathedral, where I notice the same mercs talking among each other: "I couldn't find nonthin, only cobs and shite."

Alen replied: "There was not much luck on my side either... For now, let us rest before moving on to the dungeons."

Together, they walked towards the cafeteria, allowing me to move onward and towards my study... A sight of bliss revealed to me my troubled state. Cresalin stood on the other side, waiting for me to return. She does not give me greetings through words but rather—her embrace. She held her arms around me within a tight grasp... This shocked my senses as my arms hesitated to wrap around her.

"I was worried they sealed you away..." she said, concerned.

"Not for now... They are still reluctant to find evidence."

Cresalin takes a step back and reveals her sincere smile, "I know you well, Karthuras. You would have never committed such horrible acts. My faith in you is greater than the ring hovering in the sky."

"I don't think you should regard me so highly... I am not perfect by any means—and there were choices I had to make that were questionable at best."

She placed her hand over my chest—which pounded my heart beyond its regular rate. I had to push myself away before I lost control of my rational thinking, pressing these thoughts and feelings to her in physical form. My response troubled her: "Did I do something wrong? Are you angry with me?"

I replied: "No... it's nothing. I need to focus, is all."

"Here—take this," she suddenly removes a dagger from under her mantle, "Use this when the time comes."

I took the dagger from her and was instantly reminded of that night... It was the same dagger I took from the stock room. I replied: "Thank you, Cresalin. These troubling matters have placed me in a state of desolation—but when you are beside me, there is hope in my life. One day, I shall press myself in repayment to you."

She blushed with that signature smile of hers while leaving the room. My chest aches with a foul pain once I lose sight of her. Again—I'm trapped in this perpetual state of mind. 'Parasitical' would be the best word to describe such a feeling. I wish it weren't so, but lately, her presence has gone beyond the simple concept of friendship and into the realm of romance. Alas, I'm straying far from my current situation...

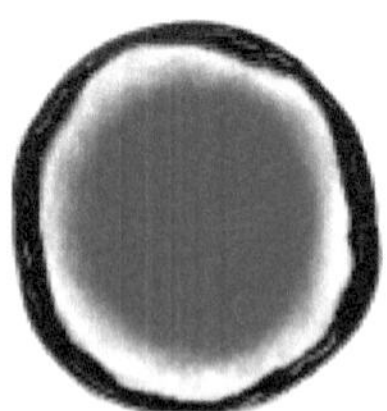

The hours dreadfully drag my patience beyond the point I will allow. Why do acts of corruption tempt me? The accusations regarding the disappearances. Horton and Dr. Krill were the only residents I had ever removed from this place. Krill was a danger to our kingdom, and Horton allowed his curiosity to place him into the clutches of that demon… I'm unsure about the others; perhaps someone here knows their whereabouts. Alen goes on and on about my deeds without any hard evidence to back him up; no—he will blame me for my wrongdoings until he convinces me that I committed these crimes. Is it possible for him to be responsible? If allowed to walk freely, I can figure this out myself. To my misfortune, I remain in the cafeteria surrounded by his mercs, who are more than willing to kill me for attempting to leave.

They talk among each other about petty discourses with a lack of self-awareness. I consider the experiment with the rat shroom, testing this very concept on humans. If Alen is why my people are disappearing, then there is no chance I will walk away, proving my innocence… At this point, I may as well wait for them to hang me outside the castle walls. There is another problem I must consider: if I were to control one of their minds, I must sacrifice the other's life, in which I'm murdering two feasibly innocent souls. I do not know what will happen to the previous host I control, but I hope they will go back to normal the next day. However, such an idea has yet to be explored.

No, it's too late now. Alen returned with a wide smirk plastered on his face. "I had caught you now, preacher," he said, amused, "I have found evidence to my accusation."

As I peered at his attire and surroundings, I could not spot this claim, so I asked, "What do you have that proves my guilt?"

He responded: "I have your journal, containing the pages that describe your actions in detail."

I reply with imposing agitation: "Journal? I had never contained one, let alone written one on its pages. I have sent letters to the Archphader and nothing more!" Truly, I had never contained my past in any journal.

Alen continues: "Let begin with the first victim, Evelyne, death from suffocation by your hands," he flips the next few pages, "Howard Poe, stabbed repeatedly outside the cathedral walls..." Again, he skips the pages, "Phader Horton, suffocated to death. Dr. Krill buried alive..." he closes the journal then crosses his arms, shaking his head with a foul smirk. "You thought of me as dull, did you Preacher?"

Never in my life have I felt this roaring fire within me... The pages detail lies of my actions! Somebody wrote these false stories to portray me as a villain. I ask Alen: "Was it you who wrote those false stories?"

He laughed: "Aw, I see—defeated as you are, you choose the path of denial and believe I am the murderer. Oh, Preacher, you have no idea how happy I am to see someone like you fall to your knees... Now, let's get this over with. Take him to the dungeon while I tend to the preparations."

This is it for me... this accusation, the politics, the anguish I had suffered through, and the past transgressions of everyone who had pushed my younger self... My patience has thinned over these past months; now, there is no reason to hold myself back. If I am to be selected as everyone's toy to discard, I shall act out my revenge accordingly—and without hesitation.

The mercs take my arms as Alen watches as I am pulled out from the door—into the main hall, then descend into the dungeon. To my fortune, he did accompany us as we traversed, thus allowing my deeds to be unseen by the common eye. I whisper: "Taketh the soul from the body—become one with the other, guiding the whims to my own," The merc on the right fainted as the other on my left was taken under my control. I demanded her to release me, then asked: "Tell me everything you know regarding Alen's intentions..."

She responded with an ominous voice, choking from the very words she spoke: "He believes Karthuras is a murderer and traitor to his people... Once he is imprisoned, a messenger will be sent to the Archphader of his transgressions. If, in any case, he does send the letter, the Archphader will return with armed guards for Karthuras's head."

From that answer, I understood the motivation, though troubling for me... The reality of this situation is that he sees me as the murderer. There are no political ties to that motion. Alas, his bias towards me will only hinder my survival. It's a shame I had to commit to this act of heresy, but like him, I wish to know the truth for myself, and the only way I can do so is by revealing the culprit who placed me in this situation. Demon—human? It matters not who; I only need an answer to this question.

Once I collected myself, I went on to see Alen again, who was no longer in the cafeteria but somewhere else within the cathedral. I kept the merc walking in front of my steed and followed behind her. Roaming the halls has become ever more tedium as I search for him. First, I entered his quarters, then went to the cellar until I returned to my study, where I heard the scribbling on the other side of the door. I glance inside, seeing him in my chair, writing a letter... I had to reframe myself from moving in too quickly; after all, that letter may be my only salvation—depending on its words and response, I may be able to... Wait a minute, if I could control his mind, my worries would be over! It's time for me to test a new theory.

I made the merc walk into the room, where Alen became disturbed and asked for a response. No response came from her lips and rather my own... And as expected from my intellect—I was right. The merc falls over lifeless as Alen stumbles for a moment until he succumbs to my mind control. I stand face to face with him now, watching the pupils slowly drift towards the back of his skull—now, I must read the letter.

To our humble Archphader, my suspicions were all true. Phader Karthuras Rotolo is the murderer, as previously stated. I hold the evidence needed to state his crimes for trial. We could end him sooner rather than later so he may be replaced instantly. With the evidence I have provided, there is little to no reason why I should delay his execution. Once you receive this letter, I demand you respond with haste!

This letter would have indeed guaranteed my death; thus, I allow the fire to consume its contents. With Alen under my control, I can rid myself of this burden and return to more critical matters... It's a shame having to end this problem through—unsavory means.

11

The nights had given me anguish as I lusted for rest... The only way I was able to—was by medicating myself by drinking liquor. Bottle—after bottle, I left on the wayside. My stomach aches with the foul crow as my mouth breaths with fire and my lungs strangle under the weight of my flesh... What am I to do with myself? What would Cresalin think of me? As I linger onto this thought without giving myself an answer—that bastard dream decisively came to me when I wanted to delay its arrival... In this dream, I awoke to a vast marble room with pillars ascending into the darkened void of the ceiling. In the middle, lower on the floor, a feminine being kneels on the ground, holding her knees. Her skin wasn't normal; instead, it was made of stone with different shades of grey. Parts of her body are chipped, exposing the pulsating red skin within. Despite her irregular appearance, I found the statue alluring to her proximity. I could hear her whispering bewildered words that were not transparent to my comprehension.

I leaned closer, seeing that smooth, unshapen face, and then I caressed the surface to see if she would give me a reaction. A reaction I did receive from her had hands that wrapped around my own... The voices sing louder and more apparent—still incoherent to grasp the words. The stone-like skin tightened around my wrist, but the touch was still soft... Attempting it was to go further into the lustful fantasies—I was sadly awakened from my own body's dogma. This bastard craves more alcohol, growing an evermore bitter taste stained against my tongue.

My servant Alen has forsaken me with his lack of—presence; thus, I take the long walk down the stairs through the halls and into the very pit of darkness. Oh—what a fool I am to have not prepared a lantern for myself... What an idiot I've become, lost in the darkness with no bottle to be seen nor felt by my hand—what a pity to turn sober amidst my state of desolation. I shall not give in just yet; there is time in this night of longing. With these hands pressed against the stone wall, I move forward until something catches my sight. At that moment, a faint light catches my wandering eye.

My vision begins to comprehend my current surroundings with help from the ignited candles. I was not alone, to my astonishment... A stranger lurks to the other side of the hallway—merging from the shadows. Though blurry, my sight remains present, and curiosity beckons me to draw closer. That dark dress was reminiscent of Cresalin's... Could this be the moment? This drunken state is not well suited for this scenario, and yet—I still want to be near her at this moment; and again, like the moron I am, my words became artful wince: "Lady of the night—sing your songs to me... For I am the wander forever moving upon the lonesome road, please allow my rest—and let us enjoy the sanctity of reunion!"

She tittered before responding to my embarrassing words: "A song I shall play for the wander if he accepts the siren's request." Her voice was strange, like Cresalin's, but the tone and emotion were absent. Alcohol is affecting my sense of awareness, sure enough.

I replied: "Maiden, I wish to hear your voice again. Tell me of this offer so I may hear you once more."

She steps closer, "Press your lips against mine and partake the sweet nectar from my body... then you will hear my voice again." I held her chin, then pressed her lips against mine. She was not hesitant to open our mouths, allowing our tongues to intertwin... Once I released myself from the addicting sensation, I then said: "I accepted your offer... May I be delighted to hear you sing?"

"Not here in the bitter cold... Take my hand and follow."

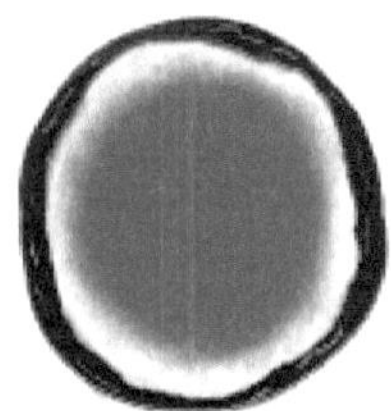

How many halls did we stroll through this extensive night? It does not matter with this stranger's soft hand wrapped against my own... How long have I had to repress these thoughts of romance? The Archphader demanded my full attention to my studies and labor, and those long hours greatly burdened this body. Yet—there was no reprieve for my efforts...

She led me inside a room of absolute radiance—décor richly scattered in velvet. My blurry visions could comprehend little at a time. Among the wall, there was a decorative frame containing a man and woman with twisted bodies that formed a single entity.

As she pressed her hands against my chest, the image of Cresalin's face suddenly became present to me... How could I not have realized it was her? That hair—that smile. A sight that gives me a reason to live… and with that beautiful dress of hers, it made my lustful eyes remain entirely still.

Awakened from that sight, I reached for her neck, licking her skin with admiration! She took every part of my soul and pressed me tightly in her body's embrace. I lifted her in my arms and tossed her on the large bed… This night will last forever, my dear—and with that heart of yours open to me, I shall fill veins with ecstasy! Thus, I ripped apart that once beautiful dress and exposed her smooth body under the crimson light… The curtains close around us unprovoked. Not even the spirits can see this mixture of flesh and pleasure. As our bodies further entangle in delight, our world shifts into a…

I let go of her as my lustful endeavors were taken in an instant. The world around me shifts from its gothic appeal to shift into the realm of depravity… The woman whom I shared this bed with was not a stranger, and neither was Cresalin. She was the same one I had met on those curious nights of desperation. I removed myself from the bed and into the slush around my feet. She rose as well and stood near me… Though pleasant her feminine figure is to behold, her smooth and stretched back skull puzzled the very nature of my intrigue.

"Why do you fear me, Karthuras?" She asked me.

I replied in awe: "I—I don't know what to say. It's hard for me to comprehend such a world—and your lack of expression!"

"This was the only way I could separate us from the mortal realm and away from 'her.'" She held my hand, "You should not fear me—for I am your sentinel through the labyrinth of madness."

Still restless, I nervously asked: "My sentinel? Was it Sleeper who sent you here to me? Or am I truly lost within the contents of my mind?"

"Sleeper has no say in this matter. I am here upon my own accord."

"No—you're just a specter. How can you help me...? And why would you!?"

She presses her hand against my chest, "Do you not feel the weight from my touch...? Here, this will prove to you that I am faithful." She unwraps a long black scarf made from cloth; engraved in its contents are red letters. She continued: "This will prove of my existence... This is the only way I can heal your anguish. When the day arises, I shall be there with you."

"You sound as if you know of my future... What are you hiding from me?"

Lips formed above her chin suddenly, and without delay, she gave me one more kiss, eventually guiding my staggered self through the door... I'm burdened with questions I demand answers to. Such an amenity will never be afforded to me.

<u>Alen's fake letter to the Archphader</u>

After these long months of boredom, I had finally found the evidence I needed for my suspicion of Karthuras. His innocence was concluded—however, the problem regarding the missing residents is still a mystery to me. Neither I nor my mercs could gather the information needed for this quandary.

- Alen Derickson, Knight of the Order.

<u>The Archphader's reply.</u>

I am glad to hear this news, Alen. I was worried my chosen had allowed that young, feeble mind to decay and rot from his negligence. Though my worries remain, Phader Horton's servants have answered my question regarding his unwarranted travels. 'The Cathedral of Vow' being his last known location... Forgive my thoughts for entering the realms of conspiracy, but I must ask you to keep a close eye on Phader Karthuras and Phader Horton. If they spire against me, I shall give you full disclosure of their execution... As you receive this letter, my advisor will be joined by an armed company as he arrives at the Cathedral for my investigation. I will ensure he is protected from harm and away from 'sweets'; I must have him entirely focused on his work, not overindulgence.

- Archphader of Erdphale

12

I had remained in my studies for a long while, pondering on my life as the troubling questions I plagued myself with. My servant Alen reminds me of my transgressions... I, however, spent these last months of winter indulging in Cresalin's company. Together, we walked for endless miles around the cathedral, immersed in dialogue regarding religion and our observations of the world around us. When the night arises, I continue with my curious adventures, practicing the art of conjuring that has left me disturbed—also intrigued to some extent... I hate to admit to my faults, but the bottle still plagues my cravings until I discover a way to remove such temptation. The black scarf... comforts me in my times of isolation, making alcohol a distant memory. I still wonder who that strange woman was and why she chose to help me, wishing I could show her my appreciation somehow.

Perhaps the company of a woman is all I truly need at this point. These days of labor are becoming the question of reason; reason to why I put myself through all this strife... In this time of need—I can hear Cresalin's footsteps. The door opens as she walks through the frame to approach my desk peculiarly, waltzing for my full attention. I reframed myself from her allure only to be pulled further into her questionable embrace.

She asks: "Why do you look away from me? Does my presence scare you...?"

I replied: "No—it's a complicated matter; I'm lost in my thoughts."

She presses her fingers against my shoulder. "But you and I had spent so much time together. What brought forth these worries?"

"I'm deeply disturbed... I shall not explain anymore, and please—let go of me." She lowers herself down to catch my distant gaze. I turned away in response.

"Why do you hate me so?" she asked solemnly.

I pushed myself away from the chair and held my tongue so I could begin to calm myself down before responding with my bad temper: "I—don't hate you, Cresalin. My worries are holding my rationality down and bringing forth my desires into the fold... But with everything that has happened to mc in the past, I don't know if I can trust you. Even now... How you show yourself to me, I'm lingering in despair."

She gives me that reassuring smile once again. "Why would you worry about such nonsense? Have I not been by your side through these many long days?"

"The days are nothing compared to my worrisome nights..." I felt her bosom against my back and her hands around my chest.

"I know of your plights, Karthuras. You allowed yourself to practice heretic ways and taste the fruits of true freedom. You had murdered those who spired against you from their ignorance..." My body became numb as my thoughts cleared in an instant. The very motion to respond became its obstacle. "Do not worry... your secrets are safe with me. As for your mind, you should not worry about it so much at once. Instead, why not devote your attention to me? Allow me to lead your thoughts and worries." She kisses my cheek and then leads her fingers against my groin.

A devious maneuver could unbind the tethers that restrain me—oh, why would I do so? My deeds lead me down this path... *I crave absolution.*

I pushed my helpless self away from Cresalin's grasp. I then wrap my hand against her throat to pull her in for a kiss. Her sweet moans entice the limbs connected to my body with an unending reluctance! I quickly picked her up and smacked her back against the stone wall. She wraps her legs around me as I lift her skirt, feeling her already exposed self. How shameful of me not to show the same courtesy... I insert myself inside as she quivers and moans with a loud echo. The pace was never ending—nor was I exhausted, oh no... She gave herself to me.

"Karthuras... give your soul to me!" She whimpers.

And thus, my anguish ends...

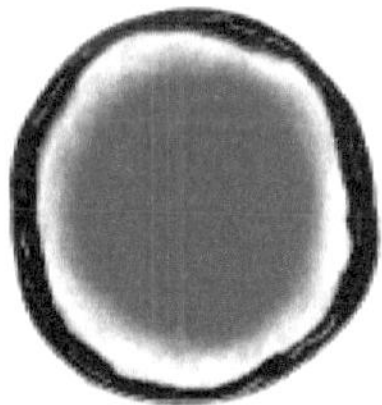

Euphoria spreads through my body—removing the burdens hindering the contemplations within my busy mind. Drowning, this sensation can be felt. I fell into that deep spiral without dreading such a fall... Cresalin finds comfort around my arms as we sleep together through the eternal dream. In my reverie—I could not see a world of beauty, just the spiral—darkness foreshadowing my end, and within that void of nothingness, my head pounds more remarkable than a hammer crashing against the sword.

My eyes open again, seeing the bottle of black liquor looming over the table, taunting me with its menacing exquisiteness. I removed the cork and then gave it a whiff, sensing the strong alcohol and—a sweet berry-like scent. Without much thought, I drank the liquid until my throat burned and my lips spurred from its bite! The taste is profoundly magnificent. I turned my gaze towards Cresalin, who was nowhere to be found... I could have sworn she was there. Aw... I see; this is a game of cat—and mouse. I shall indulge like a good participant if this is how it must be.

I tossed on my mantle and pulled up my trousers, proceeding into the halls of mind-fuckery! Step by step—staggering as a true drunkard would. Wandering until I sink further into the bottle or into the arms of that curious woman.

Whispers? Whispers I hear... I follow those curious voices emitting from behind the door. My dastardly eye peeks through the crack, and I see something I had never expected: Cresalin is sitting with Archphader's advisor, who is accompanied by a few of his knights. Why is he here? I was not given any warning of his arrival...

Cresalin told him: "Yes, I have to say these sad state of affairs are all so tragic. But I have not seen any sign of betrayal from Karthuras."

The Advisor wipes the dust from his luxurious garments as he replies: "I do not care for your wandering eyes. More—intricacies need my full attention than your care for him. He is under suspicion alongside his partner Horton, whom I have not seen yet. Come to think of it, I have not seen Alen either."

She replied: "You know Alen is well versed in his conspiracies. But I'm sure you will each other soon enough."

He stood up from his chair and carefully scratched his styled mustache, "If that is all you have to say, my dear, then this meeting is over between us. I shall have Karthuras locked up in his holding cell while you and I proceed with this search."

I pressed myself away from the door and then hurried to the nearest pillar for cover. Once they exited together, they began walking towards my bed chambers... Damn it all! Why would chaos surround me who wanted no part of it? Now, hunted as a convict, I must find a way to escape—firstly, I need to save Cresalin without killing the others. Even if they are hunting me down, I must remind myself of their ignorance of my situation. I had already caused an unfortunate situation for Alen and those mercs and—krill... No longer should I lose control of my morality, or else I am no better than the followers of Hettalies...

I will need Alen's help in this situation; however, his mental state is zombified to my whims. Could he speak similarly to his usual self? I headed to his bed chambers not far from my place of rest. I went inside with haste, seeing him standing where I had left him—troubling my thoughts became when I 'truly' see him in his current state: His eyes are sunken deeply into his skull, his limbs lacking muscle, legs shivering from his continual stance... This is unforgivable. I shall be damned in the realm of nightmares for this—as of now, the focus should turn to the others outside in the hall. To my misfortune, I hear those many steps approaching the other side of the door. Once more, I needed to hide. The only place I could take refuge was the closet, with little to no belongings inside...

The door opened as Cresalin spoke: "This is Alen's bed—" she hesitated to talk further.

"Alen?" The advisor's voice trembles as he says: "Alen, by the great ring! What has happened to you?" Everyone approaches the husk, shaking his shoulders, asking why he is stuck in his current state. "Find Karthuras—find Horton! Find those lunatics and kill them on site!"

Cresalin presses herself against the wall, allowing the three to charge out the door in their search. As she was about to join their company, she turned her gaze perfectly to mine and showed me that signature smile... I cannot concentrate. I'm... What is wrong with me? My hand opens the closet door as my legs step forward to meet with her face to face. She did not utter a single word to me, only holding my shoulder, caressing upwards to my cheek.

I... I know—my purpose now.

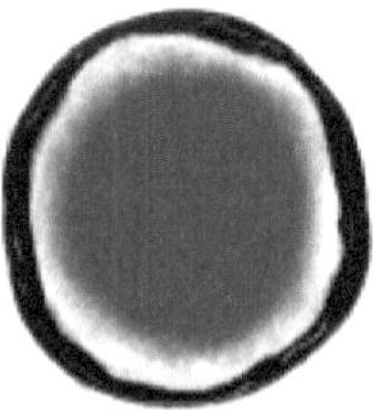

There is no longer any need to hinder my capabilities. How could I be so ignorant? True freedom was all I needed... The Archphader's Cock-sucking advisor will see the beauty of a new world; after all, he will become a pawn. Who would dare stop the very Phader who can take their life in an instant? I don't have to lift a finger to do so—only a simple collection of words is needed...

The Advisor had more knights than previously seen; they lingered outside for their orders until he gave them a new direction. Now, I sneak into the shadows and stalk around every corner. A simple dagger will not suffice in a fight – oh no! Their bulky ox-like designs will break such a weapon.

I hurried behind a group of four, then murmured: "Taketh the soul from the body—become one with the other, guiding the whims to my own." The two in the back collapsed instantly, and then I controlled the remaining... As their puppet master, I hid myself in the background, allowing these two to work for me. Their swords were drawn—blades grinding against the flesh! Such an onslaught was a beautiful sight, the compensation of torn leather blends with hissing steel. A sight of harmony to endure! When my puppets fall, I then whisper the words once more.

Blood scatters as if they were veils of decoration—as the entrails were monuments of inner beauty... I roll my eyes back from the overflow of ecstasy. I do all of this for you—my love, my inspiration... Cresalin—are you not satisfied with this display?

"*Yes—my dear Karthuras.*" Her words heal my isolation: "*But leave the advisor unharmed. Under no circumstances should you kill him. This—is to our benefit...*"

I understand, my love. There is no battle that I falter in disappointment, for the strength you give me will lead me through the very sky and into that vast silver ring.

This skirmish of mine went on for hours, and now, the Advisor is the last survivor. It's remarkable how feeble the fat man runs through these endless halls. His escape is nowhere to be seen. Alas, he still runs on – and on. Time is being wasted, my dear colleague; does he not understand the circumstances in which I'm placed? Wasting it will only hinder one's heart into a chaotic rhythm, thumping the soul from the body... What's this? He finds himself in an unfortunate place. No more turns, no more stairs, and no more rooms. A place of complete emptiness.

"Under all these predicaments, there was never an escape for you..." I said with a stern grimace.

"Kar—Karthuras... What have you done!? Why – why would you commit this atrocity?"

I replied satisfactorily: "To live in a world with absolute freedom—no more shall I stagger with numb limbs and maddening thoughts."

As I walk closer to that sniveling buffoon, Cresalin's soft hand caresses my shoulder, stopping me instantly. She said: "You have done well, my love... Let me take it from here."

Her movements towards the Advisor were like that of a predator, calculating the movement of her prey so they have no chance of escape. Suddenly, she leaps onto him, stabbing a syringe inside his neck, then injects the fluid contents. He tries to push back only to loosen his vigor within seconds until eventually falling... Once the fat man sleeps, Cresalin turns her darkened eyes to me with a beautifully long, crooked smile. She tells me, "We have only one thing left to do - till the day of reckoning arrives..." She walks to me quickly without taking more than two steps. "Kiss me—so we can begin our final trial." She opens her big mouth and then protrudes her long tongue into my mouth. Allowing me to taste the sweet nectar that puts me—into... Where...

13

I awoke in a sickly state as the cold sweat trickled down my brow—and a burning pain in my throat... Bitter my vomit was, spewing from my open lips, the black vile reeks of liquor and a substance of harsh quality—not like that of liquor, no, something beyond foul that could destroy my innards from the very scent alone. A contradiction from that sweet berry scent.

My surroundings are humid—foreboding the mind to disorientation. Barren, I am from the fragments of candlelight. The cold air does not strike great confidence within me. My mantle and trousers can only do so much in this state. The scarf wrapped around my arm is no better, just in a strange way—this piece of cloth gives me a strange comfort I had never realized before. It was as if someone was holding my arm to keep me company.

Standing here forever will not benefit my condition; thus, pressing into the unknown is my only way out or at least – my destination. Through the void, this chilling breath creeps against my exposed skin in great capacity, causing me to shiver in discontent... Nothing prepared for this instant. The flickering flames vanish, leaving me in complete darkness. Now, left with my thoughts, I wander to the conclusion of my situation. A—sort of consideration occurs; my very imagination takes the conjuring arts, morbidly using my environment as an advantage.

The stench burdens my senses, rending my ability to reason. I guide my hand forward and move closer to the source... How unfortunate I am to see it in the form: The people whom I know and spoke in dialogue are now mangled corpses rotting together like debris, ready to burn in a roaring fire. How could they have ended up in this situation? For what purpose would someone cause such a great tragedy...? No longer can I think clearly... something—something is moving within me! What damn parasite lingers within me!?

"*Use the gift, Karthuras! Raise our army!*" The voice was like mine, menacing in tone with a ghostly echo, "*Do it now! We must show Cresalin our capabilities...*"

"What are you talking about!?" I demanded to know.

"*Our purpose... She gave us this power—why waste such a gift?*"

"No—I will not practice such disgraceful acts amongst the dead. Besides..." I chuckled in an agonizing state, "Souls cannot return from Sleeper's realm."

"*This is true - body of mine, but we are not alone... Can you hear them? Scurrying around—nibbling the flesh from the rotting corpses?*"

"Damnit, who are you!?"

"*Your persistent Phantom...*"

My arms stretched forward as my lips spoke without my consent: "*Taketh the souls of rodents that scurry—allow the corpses to follow my whims!*" I could hear the many rats squeal as a collective from the sudden shock—which ended with the choking of their tongues.

The corpses malformed disturbingly into the very rodents along human parts. They stood as the limbs crackled from every inch of movement. As a single entity following my unsought demands, they move accordingly to reveal a long tunnel...

"A tunnel that will lead us to our salvation; oh Karthuras, why do you linger onto your thoughts? Why not move forward and take the steps towards true freedom?"

I can no longer think to myself...

"Thus, we walk down that long path with a warm glow against our bodies. We become decadent to its embrace—"

And in that warming aura, we emerge into the abstract display, a nightmare of a place that could only be described as such. I see figures mutilated in their physical form to become these grey beings of steel and flesh. Vibrant blue eyes that glow in the darkness brighten their path as they turn their gaze. With such a small frame they have, I'm surprised they were able to hold themselves. As a collection of tools, they move in sync, twisting levers and pressing buttons from abstract machinery... The walls are decorated with the images of a demoness guiding her hand, showing the people of the ring's destruction. Behind it—appears to be a castle, a single construct that houses the many under a single roof with a bright glowing sun behind it... As I stand here grasping the very details of my morbid surroundings, I become—I'm mortified at my position. I grasp onto the twisted pillars that reach upwards into the total darkness. I try to regain my breath, then choke from the stench of steel and rotting flesh.

"Karthuras..." Cresalin—calls for me? Her voice had shifted from its pleasant tune into something, a macabre of a song none could describe its contents. "Karthuras..." she said again, louder this time and—closer... Yes, she stands right behind me. I can sense her ominous presence, and by the great ring, I could never turn myself around to see her. I fear of her identity, who she truly is...

A beautiful sight she is, body of mine. Turn to her. See the woman who we will embrace for all of eternity...

My body moves from the voice in my head, showing my gaze to the demoness before me. No longer was she the sweet woman I once knew – and now, a being of foul creation: Her height is beyond my own; to her, I seem more like a child than a man. Her face drips down like wax warmed from the flame, with a slight open slit where she can open her mouth. Her eyes fall deep into the darkness of her skull's sockets, not allowing me to see the pupils, its colorful oval. Her long-shriveled arms extended towards me with long feminine fingers, crookedly twisting and bent uncannily. The details of her appearance brought forth a memory that I fear to be true...

She said, "You have already discovered more than my previous apprentice... I was right to have sent that letter to the Archphader regarding your involvement."

"W-what?" I quivered in response.

"The young are always willing to work hard and learn quickly. My incentive, Cresalin, gave you the proper motivation to strive forward and become who you are now."

I press my back against the pillar, hiding my fearful expression by hovering my hand to the front. Then I reply: "Hettalies... All this time, I spoke to you—falling in love to the extent I could only describe as an obsession! How—how could I be so blind!?"

"This feeling will only last in the short-term, my love... Come," she pressed her long fingers against my shoulder, then guided me through the vast space. My eyes could not stop looking at the grotesque things moving and working the machine in ways of torment. Like stabbing the very chest of one's enemy or perhaps the strangling of necks. The steel bounds with the intestines to connect separate parts that flow a blood current from one part to the next... I feared questioning the purpose they served, knowing deep down it would be used for malignant means.

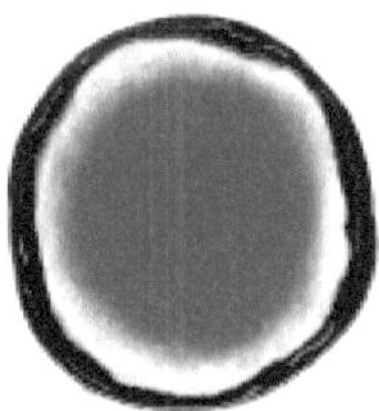

Hettalies led me down a narrow path of interconnecting tunnels with scattered carts containing stones and ore. The blue eyes of beaming light from the creatures became our only light source, their gazes pointing out the details by turning their heads. She tells me, "You are well-versed in my history... but do you know my true reason for being in this world?"

I replied: "Not that I can recall besides the common. You are our sworn protector."

"Sleeper indeed placed me onto this world for that reason, but there was more to it... He wanted me to create beings in his new – ideal world. Such a precise creation took time and effort. First, I combine both human steels into one mesh. It's a shame the body could not handle such insertions. That's when I had to give them the gift all demons have, 'Immortality.' Of course, I could not allow them to have free thought, so I had their brains taken from their very skulls, thus answering their steel helms and covered expressions."

"This new world—why would he care for a new creation if willing to leave us behind? Would he not care again?"

She replied: "This world is nothing more than a breeding ground for his future creations. Once I have given him the proper tools to create a new breed of life form, he will allow me complete control of this world..."

We enter a hollow room lit by the ignited cauldrons around us. The structures were twisted and turned into ways that questioned its intent. Rigged edges that will cut the very hand that dares touch its foul design. At the very end, a wall of machinery is littered with parts and tools that turn my stomach in foul directions, my imagination being the culprit to such pain...

She continued: "My true form may not be pleasurable to your lustful eyes and so—" her body morphs into Cresalin's form, "I can shift into the woman you desired," she smiled gleefully and expressed herself in a charming posture. "Admittedly, I would not mind allowing you to take me in your demon form, throwing and using me to your heart's content! And when you get bored of my beauty," She shifts back into her demon self, "You can then indulge yourself in the innards of demon flesh..."

I took a step back and held my breath from the display, and her words made me question: "My—demon form?"

"Yes, I cannot have a mortal by my side with his limitations. I need you to become something more, someone who is callous – full of hatred, disregards empathy in the pursuit of pleasure and power. Your morals hinder such capabilities, which is why I had to inject you with that parasite."

"So, this is where it all ends for me?" I uttered in despair.

"Do not sound so pathetic! You will become something more to me..." She waves her hand, gesturing for those things to take hold of me. I did not resist, nor did I have the strength. She continued: "Once this is over, you will learn to thank me—if not I, then—" She unveils the black cloth over her belly, showing me... showing me the—bulge inside her belly, "For our child who will be the first to spawn from a demon..."

My head turns away in despair... My child will be born into this maddening world as I become a foul being, corrupted by the demoness in front of me. They drag me away as I yell foully from the top of my lungs and into this hollow room! They bound steel against my limbs, clothes ripped and cut off from my body except—the scarf? They could not remove its binding around my arm. It tightens against my flesh, never wanting to let go of me... They gave up on its removal, then took upon the tools from the wall, then directed those rigged edges towards my exposed body! It turns in a continuous circular motion with a loud hiss screeching in my ears. When it touches my skin—I fall into a deep slumber...

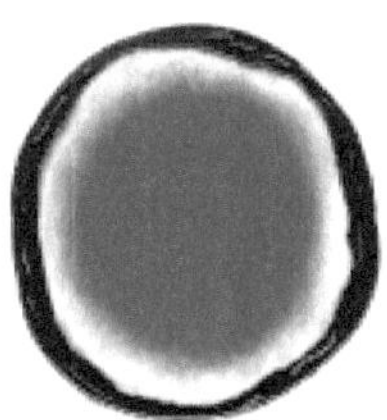

I awaken to a dark sky with crimson-shaded stars flickering into the great beyond. My head is on a soft lap with a black dress over the skin... This comfort is unimaginable, and that sense of fear is no longer present. I look at the stranger who holds me in her embrace, being the one who had given me this scarf, the faceless woman. She looks down at me with her smooth face, using her gentle hands to rub the sides of my head slowly. "Do not fret, Karthuras. For I am here with you during your troubling times..." Her voice—is angelic, a sweet tune that puts my mind into a euphoric state.

I ask her: "Why would you care for a stranger like me who has never once spoken to you?"

"Our souls have bounds to those around us that none can explain their purpose... The demon had poisoned you with her potions that swayed away my guiding hand; it's a shame I could not save you from the many lies. Perhaps it was for the best..."

"Why so?"

"In your current form, you cannot fight her—nor her followers. No sword can cut the very soul from her shell... However, this was your only chance for salvation. As long as my scarf remains whole, I shall remain by your side until the end of time."

I questioned: "I can't believe in your existence... After dealing with these horrible past encounters, I created you out of need for my persistence... How can any of this be real? How would I know you are a true being and not part of my imagination?"

"Would you rather remain in total isolation...?" I did not give her a response. "Then let us take part in this relief—and enjoy the scenery together."

I gaze upon the void once more – the dark beauty of it all conflicts with my thoughts. I felt compelled to ask for her name, but she did not reply with one nor give me a reason to remain silent... instead, she continued to comfort me. I am perplexed at the idea of this woman being an actual entity, not a trick of my reality.

As I lay here, waiting for my life to end. I am left with this final thought: "The very concept of 'love' is a tragic comedy. A questionable substance is portrayed in ways of mannerism; I am a fool to believe in its existence. As for isolation, there is honesty in silence—and no more lies whispered to my ears..."

Don't miss out!

Visit the website below and you can sign up to receive emails whenever Landon Cook publishes a new book. There's no charge and no obligation.

https://books2read.com/r/B-A-MWMN-UELDD